"Loss sneaks up on you, you know?"

A single tear streaked down Eve's face. She stared into the darkness. "I've been just trying to survive these last few years. Being here, it's like having time to finally breathe."

She looked at Tanner then. The honesty in her eyes sliced deep. Still, he hesitated. Talking about his feelings wasn't exactly his strong suit. "Sometimes I think I only went on for other people, Eve. My brothers."

"And now?"

He wanted to end this conversation that was casting light into places that were better off in the dark. But he couldn't do that, not when Eve was being open with him.

Her hand slid into Tanner's, fingers warm as she tangled them with his. They didn't move.

And for a moment, it was as if they were the only two people in the world. There was no today or tomorrow, or even ten minutes from now. There was only this moment with the swing rocking and Christmas music playing…

Award-winning author **Stephanie Dees** lives in small-town Florida with her pastor husband and their two youngest children. A Southern girl through and through, she loves sweet tea, SEC football, corn on the cob and air-conditioning. For further information, please visit her website at stephaniedees.com.

A Daughter
for Christmas

Stephanie Dees

LOVE INSPIRED
INSPIRATIONAL ROMANCE

LOVE INSPIRED®
INSPIRATIONAL ROMANCE

Recycling programs for this product may not exist in your area.

ISBN-13: 978-1-335-48858-9

A Daughter for Christmas

This edition published by arrangement with Harlequin Books S.A.

For questions and comments about the quality of this book, please contact us at CustomerService@Harlequin.com.

Love Inspired
22 Adelaide St. West, 40th Floor
Toronto, Ontario M5H 4E3, Canada
www.Harlequin.com

Printed in U.S.A.

To appoint unto them that mourn in Zion, to give unto them beauty for ashes, the oil of joy for mourning, the garment of praise for the spirit of heaviness; that they might be called trees of righteousness, the planting of the Lord, that he might be glorified.

—*Isaiah* 61:3

For Sierra Donovan, best critique partner
and friend a writer could hope for.
Here's to all the chapters to come!

Acknowledgments

Thanks to Melissa Jeglinski
at The Knight Agency and Melissa Endlich
at Love Inspired—you're the best!

And a special thanks to T and S,
who never fail to prop me up,
and who make this solitary life a lot more fun!

Chapter One

Christmas music drifted out of the open door of the small cabin as Eve Fallon tied the last piece of garland to the porch with a flourish. Three hours after arriving, with her minivan still loaded down with boxes, she wasn't even going to pretend that she wouldn't rather be unpacking in the kitchen. But these decorations weren't for her.

They were for four-year-old Alice, who was dancing around Eve on her tiptoes, the expression on her sweet little face the closest thing to a smile that Eve had seen in a long time.

Eve held the end of an extension cord and the garland. "Ready?"

Alice gave a vigorous nod, silky blond curls bouncing.

"Well, okay, then." With a laugh, Eve pushed the cords together. The lights sparked to life in the dark green garland. Every last one of them. A Christmas dream come true.

"Ohh," Alice breathed.

Eve looked at her in surprise. "You like it?"

"Pretty."

Tears sprang into Eve's eyes. "It is, baby. It is pretty."

The single word was the first Alice had said in six long weeks, since her preschool had been locked down and the little girl had witnessed her teacher being held at gunpoint by an estranged boyfriend.

No telling what would have happened if he hadn't gotten spooked by police sirens before running out the back door. Eve shook her head. No good came from speculating about that.

Brushing her hands off on her jeans, she smiled at her daughter. "Why don't we go see what we can do with the rest of this place? I heard there was a Christmas tree in the bedroom closet. Want to see if we can find it?"

As Alice ran back through the door, Eve took a moment to look around. The tiny cabin was tucked into the back of a tranquil farm. She'd rented it on a whim, deciding she and Alice needed to get out of the city, away from the memories that locked Alice behind a wall of fear.

A fresh start. A chance to heal.

Inhaling a deep breath of crisp December air, she nodded. Moving to Alabama had been the right decision. The cozy scent of smoke from nearby fireplaces wafted on the air. It even smelled like Christmas here.

Laughing to herself, Eve turned toward the house and her little girl. Alice loved Christmas. And Eve would do just about anything to make Alice feel happy and safe again.

"Hey!"

Eve spun toward the voice. The owner of said voice

was tall and lean, looked to be about thirty-five or so, with a dusty leather cowboy hat on his head. And as he strode toward her, she could see a day or two of stubble shadowing a strong jaw.

She smiled. "Hi."

"You're trespassing." Dark eyes narrowed as he glowered at her.

Her smile faded. "Excuse me?"

When his expression didn't change, she realized this wasn't going to be the welcome she'd been expecting. Reaching behind her, she tugged the door closed and prayed Alice didn't come outside. The last thing her daughter's fragile confidence needed was an encounter with an angry man.

"You're trespassing." He said it slower, as if she didn't understand him the first time.

Eve met him at the bottom of the steps and held out a hand. "Ah, no. I'm Eve Fallon. The tenant."

"We don't have a tenant." He still didn't smile. And up close, she realized that his face was less angry than exhausted. And something else…sad?

"Beg to differ." Keeping him in sight, Eve walked to her van. She picked up a file folder from the front seat, flipped through it and pulled out the stack of papers she was looking for. She held it out for him. "I have a lease. It's signed by—"

He tugged the papers from her hand and scowled at the signature. "Garrett. I'm gonna kill him."

She took a step backward toward the house, her hand groping for the porch railing behind her. "I think you need to leave now."

His face changed, the harsh lines softening. He took

a step away from her, one hand coming up, her lease still clenched in the other. "You don't have to be scared. I won't hurt you. I'm leaving."

Eve believed he was telling the truth. Regardless, she watched him until he rounded the corner and walked slowly toward the main farmhouse. Her shoulders—and her mood—deflated like a three-day-old balloon.

Okay, so maybe the new place wasn't as perfect as she imagined it would be. She'd dealt with worse. But it was disappointing. This was supposed to be her refuge, the place where Alice turned back into the happy preschooler she'd been before the armed intruder threatened her school.

Eve took a deep breath, searching the clear blue sky for inspiration. *Lord, what do I do now?*

First, she needed to check on Alice. If that man had scared Alice...well, Eve wasn't about to let a cranky cowboy retraumatize her little girl.

She found the four-year-old on the yellow-flowered couch that had come with the place. Alice was bent over her iPad, noise-canceling headphones covering her ears, but she looked up as the door opened. A fleeting smile for her mom, then she turned her attention back to the game.

Eve let out a long, slow breath. Thankfully, no damage done. Yet. Annoyance merged with a healthy dose of anger as she dug her cell phone out of her back pocket and dialed her landlord with shaking fingers.

He could figure this mess out. She had a Christmas tree to decorate.

Tanner Cole paced the length of the farmhouse porch and back again, waiting for his brother to pick up the phone. He'd been drilling the importance of owning your mistakes into that knucklehead for years. Seemed only fair he'd have to own his own now, for the kind of welcome he'd given the new tenant.

With an impatient gesture, he pulled off his hat, scrubbed a hand over his hair and settled it back where it belonged. Grief lay heavy on his shoulders today, reminders everywhere of the life he'd lost, especially at the cottage.

He'd carried Kelly over the threshold of that door when they'd returned from their honeymoon. And carried their son over it when they'd arrived home from the hospital ten months later. The memories were vivid in his mind, as if the car accident had happened yesterday, not fifteen years ago today.

They were with him every day, but he didn't dwell on the loss, not anymore. One day a year he let himself get angry that in an instant he'd lost so much that mattered to him. Both of his parents, Kelly, little Caleb. He owed it to them—all of them—to grieve.

Garrett answered the phone with a clipped "Well?"

Tanner stopped walking. "I may have messed up."

His brother let the silence stretch on, one of his lawyer tricks that managed to simultaneously convey both shock and judgment at Tanner's actions. It was designed to make Tanner want to say something—anything—to fill the void.

"If you have something to say to me, spit it out." Tanner scowled, and when Garrett's silence continued, he doubled down on his annoyance. "You should've told me you leased the cottage."

Papers rustled as Garrett shuffled them on his desk. "We talked about listing it at the last family meeting."

"Listing it, not that it had actually been rented." Tanner caught himself and took a breath, scratching his forehead. He was in the wrong here. Not Garrett. Not the new tenant. "It doesn't matter. I was a jerk to her. It's a bad day, but that's no excuse."

Garrett sighed. "I know. And for what it's worth, I'm sorry. I thought she was moving in over the weekend."

"Kelly would skin me alive if she knew how I'd acted." The afternoon sun had warmed the chill out of the air, and Tanner shrugged out of his flannel shirt, wadding it up and tossing it onto a porch chair. "And Mom…she'd be slamming things around in the kitchen, trying to get her point across."

Garrett swallowed hard on the other end of the phone call. "Mom never hesitated to bang a pan if she thought it would help. I miss them."

There was a catch in his brother's voice. And the heavy weight of grief lifted slightly for Tanner, just remembering his brother shared it, understood it. "Me, too. I'm sorry about the tenant. I think I scared her."

"You're gonna have to apologize. We need the income. It isn't much, but she signed a lease, and we already allocated the money for the new barn."

"I'd apologize anyway. You know that," Tanner said, back stiffening.

"I know you would." A sigh came through the line, muffled voices behind it. "My next appointment is here. I'll see you on Saturday for family dinner. Fix this, Tanner."

"I'm on it."

Garrett's wife, Abby, had started the Saturday tradition as a way to reconnect. Tanner, who valued his alone time, had privately balked at the idea. Weren't they under each other's feet enough as it was?

But his younger brothers' wives had brought laughter and music and children back into the old farmhouse. New enthusiasm for their business. And it didn't take Tanner long to realize Abby had been right. He'd spent a lot of years barely surviving. He needed his nieces and nephew with their sloppy kisses and their toys underfoot and all their noise to remind him he was alive.

Remind him he *wanted* to be alive.

He picked up his flannel shirt off the rocking chair and took it into the house, hanging it on a hook by the door.

His dog, Sadie, padded over to him from her bed by the fireplace. He reached down to scratch her head before continuing through the living room to the kitchen, where he poured himself a cup of coffee.

Sadie tilted her head, making one brown rottweiler eyebrow seem higher than the other. Tanner felt the ghost of a smile tug the corners of his mouth despite himself. "No comments from you, thanks."

He set his cup on the table and picked up his pencil to start a list. He had a feeling he was going to need every advantage he could scrounge up to make amends with the new tenant.

And everyone knew apologies went better with presents.

With Alice in bed in the tiny second bedroom, Eve picked up a soft wool throw, wrapped it around her shoulders and stepped onto the porch. The twinkle lights she'd hung earlier were friendly and homey, but it was the stars in the sky that made her catch her breath. She never would've seen these in Atlanta and they were glorious, as if God had taken His paintbrush and flicked it, slinging stars into a random, beautiful pattern across the sky.

Rustling dry leaves caught her attention. She'd heard coyotes howling in the distance earlier. She took a step closer to the house. They didn't have coyotes in the city.

A huge black dog took the stairs in one bounding leap. Eve jumped back. "Oh!"

"Sadie!" A man's voice called in the distance.

"You're Sadie, I presume?" Eve took a deep breath, laughing a little at her groundless fears…now that she knew they were groundless.

The dog nosed her hand for a scratch. And who could resist that soulful, dark-eyed gaze? Eve dropped into a chair and scratched the big black head as her new neighbor rounded the corner of the dirt road that led from his house to hers.

She sighed. He might be grumpy, but he was also handsome, effortlessly masculine in his jeans and boots. But honestly, she wasn't up to another confrontation.

He stopped when he caught sight of her. "I should've known Sadie would find you."

"She's sweet." Eve watched as the dog unerringly sniffed her way to a cookie Alice had dropped under the porch swing that afternoon. "Is there something I can do for you?"

"I come in peace." His eyes on her, he smiled slightly and lifted a basket. "Bearing gifts?"

"Well, in that case, by all means…" She waved an arm at the porch.

The man wasn't as presumptuous as his dog, stopping at the bottom of the steps. "I was a jerk this morning. No excuses. I hope you can forgive me."

Eve brushed spiky brown bangs away from her eyes and leaned forward to study his face. "Did your brother make you say that?"

"He might've encouraged me." A dimple deepened in his cheek as he took a step forward and held out his hand. "I'm Tanner Cole."

"Eve Fallon." She reached her hand out to his, her eyes darting up as strong fingers, work worn and calloused, closed over hers.

"I remember. And who is that little towhead in the window?"

"What?" Eve spun around in her chair, catching a glimpse of her wide-eyed four-year-old staring out at them. "Hang on just a minute."

When Eve opened the door, Alice was still at the window, bare feet poking out from the hem of her ruffled pink nightgown. Her eyes were worried and full of questions as she pointed at Tanner.

Eve lifted Alice into her arms, nuzzling the curls that smelled like baby shampoo from an earlier bath. "It's okay, baby girl. He lives in the big white house down the road. As long as you're awake, why don't you come say hello?"

She tucked the warm throw around Alice before walking back out to the porch, where Tanner still waited at the bottom of the steps. "This towhead is my daughter, Alice. She's four."

"Hi, Alice. I'm Tanner." He waggled the fingers of one hand and hefted the large basket again with the other. "I brought you all some presents from all of us here at Triple Creek Ranch. Do you like cookies?"

Eve felt Alice's little body tremble as she buried her face in Eve's shoulder. "She definitely likes cookies, but she's not much for strangers. Sorry."

"It's okay. She's not being rude. She doesn't know me." Tanner's smile was open and easy as he placed the basket within their reach on the porch and carefully stepped back. "I loaded the basket up with some of the stuff we stock at our farm stand. Everything's organic and made right here."

"That's very nice of you. Thank you."

He gave her a single nod and took a step back. "I'll see you around, then. Come on, Sadie."

The dog was at his side in an instant, and he turned to walk away.

"I'm sorry about your family," Eve blurted, immediately wishing she could grab the words and shove them back in.

Tanner's footsteps faltered to a stop, but he turned back, hands in his jeans pockets. "Thanks."

"Your brother told me. He thought it might explain… you know, what happened earlier. I wish I'd known. Anniversaries are hard." She'd learned that firsthand after her husband hadn't come home after his last deployment. The empty spaces could never be filled. You just kept living with them day by day until they became a part of who you were.

"Still no excuse for rudeness. But thank you for your kindness." His eyes were shadowed, and she felt an ache in her throat as she held his gaze.

Tanner smiled. "I'll see you tomorrow. It was nice meeting you both."

He turned to walk away, the dog loping along beside him. They'd been so young—Garrett and Devin in middle school, Tanner barely twenty-one. He would've had to be strong to keep his brothers together after losing their parents, especially while dealing with such a tragic blow himself. Strong in another way to admit he was wrong today and apologize.

Eve hefted the large basket to her hip, her eye catching on a jar of what looked like dried herbs and flowers, a handwritten note tied around the top. *Chamomile and spearmint tea. Good for muscles sore from moving.*

She smiled to herself. Sweet gesture, one that belied that imposing exterior. The contradictions intrigued her. Not in *that* way, of course. Maybe he had rugged good looks. And maybe she'd felt something when she put her hand in his. So what?

He showed no sign of being interested, and she had no time for relationships or dates and such even if he was. Her hands were full running her small home business and being a single mom to Alice.

So that settled that. But, she thought, as she tucked Alice back into bed, she could use a friend. And it seemed like maybe Tanner Cole could use one, too.

Chapter Two

When Tanner came into the farmhouse to wash up after chores the next morning, the delicious aroma of cookies baking drew him to the kitchen. His sister-in-law Lacey was slowly adding flour to the commercial-size mixer they'd invested in last year as demand from the farm stand had grown. "Wow, I missed you guys."

"You missed my cooking? You're more desperate than I thought."

"I missed my daily quota of cookies, for sure, and Devin's help with the chores, but it was too quiet around here with you two in Oklahoma. I know your dad enjoyed some time with you, though."

"He did. And Devin made some good contacts. Turns out more than a few people buy an unbroken horse and have no idea what to do with it. It's a good thing we're building a new barn. We're going to need it." Lacey's hands never slowed as she rolled the dough. "I heard we have a new renter in Garrett's cottage. What's she like?"

Tanner thought of Eve, the wide green eyes that

seemed to understand so much. The kindness she'd shown to him even though he'd been less than welcoming. "She's nice. And she has a little girl who's four."

"Aww. I'll have to go by and say hello when I get caught up." Thirteen-month-old Phoebe pulled up on Lacey's leg with a cranky cry. Her face was red and streaked with tears. Lacey glanced down. "*If* I ever get caught up."

"I've got her. Just let me wash my hands."

Lacey sent him a harried smile. "She wants milk, but she still won't take a sippy cup. I'll grab her a bottle as soon as I get this batch cut and in the oven. Our supplies for the farm stand are dangerously low."

"Want me to get the milk?"

"Yes, please. Give me a minute to actually get something accomplished?" Lacey brushed loose tendrils of hair away from her eyes with a weary forearm.

Phoebe's twin brother, Eli, was in the high chair finger painting with what Tanner was reasonably sure was banana yogurt. When he looked closer, he realized most of the yogurt had ended up in Eli's hair. "Um, Lacey?"

When she glanced up, he realized she looked more tired than normal mom-with-toddler-twins tired. Her eyes were dark with shadows, face pale with fatigue. They'd gotten home in the middle of the night, so maybe it was just that. He smiled. "Never mind, I got it."

She reached to dump a spoon in the sink and missed, the spoon clattering to the floor. She swayed, her fingers grasping for the edge of the countertop.

"Lacey!" Panic rose, a flash flood in a dry gulch. He snaked an arm out, catching her before she could crumple and guided her into a kitchen chair. "Don't move. I'll call Devin."

"Don't." Her voice was wan, but firm. "Please?"

Lacey gulped air, her head drooped over, dark hair hiding her face.

Pulling his phone from his back pocket, Tanner keyed in a text. He filled a glass of water and placed it in front of her before reaching down for little Phoebe, who was still crying.

When the front door flew open, Lacey sighed.

"Sorry," Tanner muttered. He left her sitting there and met Devin in the living room. "She almost passed out in the kitchen."

"Lace?" Devin rushed into the kitchen. Tanner heard Eli's squeal of joy when he saw his dad and the indignant protest when Devin instead went to Lacey. "Hon? You okay?"

Tanner wasn't sure what to do. He glanced down at Phoebe, who'd nestled in and fallen asleep almost as soon as he'd picked her up. There was probably some rule about timing of naps and all that stuff, but if so, he didn't know what it was. He walked her back to the sunny yellow room she shared with Eli and placed her in the crib, glad that for the time being Lacey and Devin were still living in the farmhouse while building their house. They'd still be close, just beyond the pond, on the back forty acres, but still.

Back in the living room, Tanner saw that Devin had moved Lacey to sit on the sofa. Tanner jerked a thumb toward the kitchen, where Eli was crying. "I'll get Eli."

"Thanks." Devin didn't look up from Lacey's face. She was pale. Too pale.

"Hey, little buddy. Did you think we all left you alone?" In the kitchen, Tanner reached for the latches on the high chair tray and then remembered the yogurt. "One second."

He took a dish towel from the drawer next to the sink and held it under the water. Devin walked into the room, saw the wet rag in Tanner's hand and took it. "Thanks."

"She okay?"

Devin shrugged, but his face was serious. "I think so. She says she's been feeling off the last few days. Maybe all the travel?"

"Maybe."

Devin hesitated. "If she can get an appointment at the doctor this morning, do you think you can watch the kids?"

"Of course." As a rule, his brothers, Devin and Garrett, tried to avoid asking for his help with their babies. Tanner guessed they figured maybe it would remind him of what he'd missed with his own.

And maybe he used to think that, too, but the truth was, nothing would make him miss Caleb less. Instead, being able to help with his nieces and nephew made him feel more needed. More a part of things.

Tanner frowned at the running water, pulled another towel out and wet it. Once he'd squeezed it out, he turned back to Eli, who'd stopped crying and was watching him with a wary expression. "Yeah, you're not going to like this."

He managed to get most of the yogurt off Eli with one large swipe. Before the little dude could even get a good yell going, Tanner unhooked the high chair tray and picked him up.

"We're heading out," Devin called back from the living room.

"Keep me posted." Tanner walked through the door with Eli just in time to catch a glimpse of Lacey's scowl.

"I'm not sick, Devin. Seriously. I need to make cookies."

"The cookies can wait till later." Devin opened the door, and she walked through it.

Tanner looked down at Eli. "Well, dude, it looks like it's you and me. Let's see what we can get into."

He watched from the front door as Devin pulled away from the house with Lacey in the front seat of their crew-cab pickup truck. She might protest all the way to the doctor, but Devin's face was carved into worried lines. They'd all experienced so much loss. They needed to know she was okay.

A pudgy baby fist grabbed his nose, forcibly pulling Tanner from his own worried thoughts, and he chuckled. "We can handle things here. Right, Eli?"

From inside the house in the direction of the nursery, he heard a wail.

Maybe he'd spoken too soon. He cracked open the door to the nursery. Phoebe was standing in the bed, her face scrunched up and damp with tears.

He looped one arm around her and hoisted her into his arms, opposite Eli. She stuck her thumb in her mouth, her eyes suspicious.

"No worries, munchkin. Uncle Tanner knows where the bottles are. And then we'll go outside." There. A plan. He totally had this.

Eve meandered down the road that, from all appearances, ran straight down the middle of the farm.

Fields stretched out alongside the road, cows on one side and wildflowers on the other. It was beautiful. Peaceful. And maybe it was silly, but she felt like she could breathe better here than she could in the city.

And maybe she just wanted to believe it, but Alice seemed to feel a little bit lighter, too. The four-year-old ran a few steps ahead, Sadie the rottweiler trotting along beside her. When Eve opened the front door early this morning, Sadie had been lying on the mat, waiting. She'd nosed her way into the house and lain on the floor by Alice's bed.

Since Alice woke, the two had been inseparable. Eve had even heard Alice humming as she played with her paper dolls, Sadie right beside her on the rag rug. It wasn't healing, not yet, but it was a start.

At some point, though, Tanner would be looking for his dog. Eve figured it would be better if they found him first, rather than him coming to the cottage. The memory of her blurted sentiment about his family made her cheeks heat even as it came to mind now.

She could hear the baby squeals before she could see the babies making them. If she remembered right, one of the Cole brothers had twins. "You hear the babies, Alice?"

The little girl nodded, her eyes sparkling.

"It sounds like their mom has them outside. Let's go see." But when the farmhouse came in sight, it was Tanner outside underneath a huge oak tree pushing two toddler swings hanging from one of the large lower branches. As the twins would swing toward him, he'd try to grab a foot and they would go into gales of giggles.

"That looks like a fun game," Eve said as they approached the swings.

"It is, for them. You'd think they'd get tired of it, but no, they don't." Tanner smiled, a hint of amusement playing around his lips as he nipped one of the babies out of a swing. "I wondered where my dog wandered off to."

"I have no idea why, but she was waiting outside my door this morning. She and Alice are now firm friends."

Alice unearthed a ball from the flower bed and threw it for Sadie, who loped after it, picked it up and returned to drop it at Alice's feet. The little girl patted Sadie's head and tossed the ball again.

"See what I mean?"

Tanner shrugged. "Sadie has kind of a sixth sense for people and animals. Maybe she thinks your daughter could use some extra love with the move and all."

"Maybe." It was a startling thought. But maybe Sadie did sense that Alice was fragile and needed a friend. Changing the subject, she said, "Niece and nephew?"

"Yep, the one in the swing is Phoebe. And this is Eli." He indicated the baby in his arms. "He's not a fan of Uncle Tanner on a good day." As if to emphasize the point, Eli scowled and let out a grumpy sigh.

With a laugh, Eve held her arms out. "Can I try? I love babies."

"Yes, please." He handed him over to Eve. "I'm a little out of my depth with both of them. Lacey wasn't feeling well, so Devin took her to the doctor."

"Oh, I'm sorry. Is there anything I can do?"

"You're doing it. These guys are off their nap schedule and I think Eli's ready for a break, but Phoebe won't let me put her down so I can get him to sleep," he said, taking the second twin out of her swing. They walked to the front porch of the farmhouse.

"Garrett mentioned they've been on a trip, too. I remember when Alice was a baby, traveling was a nightmare." While they chatted, Eve kept her eye on the four-year-old, who was jumping from the bottom step to the ground over and over again, a look of intense focus on her face.

"But you…" Tanner shook his head slightly as he shifted the baby to the other arm. "Never mind. None of my business."

"But I had Alice's dad with me then?" Eve guessed that's what he'd been about to say. "It's okay. I don't mind talking about it. He was in the army. Alice was born while he was overseas."

He'd gone very still, his dark eyes on her, face carved into granite-hard lines. "He didn't come back?"

"No, he did. Physically, at least." She looked down at the baby in her arms. Eli was heavy, a limp, sleepy weight. All she could see of him was the profile of his chubby toddler cheek.

Alice had wandered across the lane to pick the wildflowers—weeds, really—that grew around the base of the fence posts. "I think it must be very hard to go from being a war fighter to dirty diapers, nighttime feedings, TV on the couch. Brent tried, but he just couldn't make it work. After some time with us, he moved back to his parents' home. Six months later, he re-upped. He was killed in action less than a month later."

Tanner was quiet for a long minute, her words floating in the air between them. As the silence stretched, she opened her mouth to reassure him that it was fine. *She* was fine. But then he spoke.

"Last night when you said anniversaries are hard, you were speaking from personal experience." It wasn't a question.

She nodded slowly. "I truly didn't mean to compare what you went through to my life. But I do understand, at least a little bit."

That dent in his cheek deepened. "So what brought you to Red Hill Springs?"

"Alice had a traumatic experience a couple of months ago. I thought a change of scenery would do her good. And Brent's parents live about an hour away. They adore her, and it'll be nice to have the support."

A shiny black truck drove in and pulled to a stop in the driveway. Alice ran back to Eve, attaching herself to Eve's leg. Eve cupped Alice's head, tousled her hair and reminded herself that slow progress was still progress.

A petite woman wearing jeans and a T-shirt slid out of the passenger side. Her long brown hair was in a braid that fell over one shoulder.

The man who got out of the driver's side had to be Tanner's younger brother Devin. He stepped out from behind the door, and she realized he walked with a cane.

Tanner quickly introduced Devin and Lacey to Eve before he focused a look on Devin. "Everything okay?"

Devin looked down at his wife with a smile. "Everything okay, honey?"

Lacey sighed and pulled a thin slip of paper out of her pocket. She held it out to Tanner. He stared at it.

Eve smothered a laugh. She knew what that grainy picture meant.

"Need me to translate?" Devin's grin grew wider. He pointed. "That little blob right there is a baby."

Eyes wide, Tanner stuttered out his congratulations before hugging Lacey. "Are you happy?"

"Shell-shocked. Scared, a little. You know my body doesn't much like being pregnant."

Devin took Phoebe out of Tanner's arms and blew kisses into her cheek before settling her in the crook of his arm. "The doctor said Lacey's going to have to take it easy, especially for the next month or two."

Lacey was already shaking her head. "I don't have time for taking it easy. I have thirteen-month-old twins. The farm stand to bake for. Not to mention the big Christmas party we're having for the foster kids. It's only a month away."

"We may have to let go of some things, Lacey." When she scowled, Devin shrugged. "Just being realistic, honey."

"Be realistic about something else. We're *not* giving up the party."

"I can help." Eve heard the words come out of her mouth. She felt just as surprised as the three faces looked as they swung simultaneously toward her. She was almost positive they'd forgotten she was standing there.

Tanner shook his head. "We'll figure something out."

Devin snorted. "You're not exactly full of Christmas spirit."

Crossing his arms, Tanner ignored his brother. "We'll figure something out."

Eve shrugged, with a smile. "I was an event planner, before—well, before. Plus, a party for foster kids sounds like something I'd want to help with anyway. You guys think about it and let me know. I'm gonna head back to the cottage and get supper started for me and Alice."

Gently, she transferred a sleeping Eli to Lacey's arms. "I'm happy for you guys, and it's really nice to meet you both." To Alice, she said, "Come on, sweet girl."

As they walked toward the cottage, Sadie fell into step beside Alice. Eve stopped. "Sadie, go back."

She started walking again. Sadie started walking, too, keeping pace beside them.

Eve turned back to Tanner, throwing her hands up.

"I don't mind if she goes with you, as long as you don't. She'll come home when she's ready."

Alice tugged at Eve's hand. "Please?"

The voice was as soft as a feather, but Eve heard it. How could she say no? "Okay, then. I guess we have a guest for supper."

Alice's face lit up, and Eve laughed. She glanced back as she turned the corner toward the cottage. Lacey and Devin each had one of the twins in their arms. Tanner was standing with them, but slightly off to the side, and she wondered if he felt that distance.

What would it be like to have lost your family and watch as your brothers found theirs? He was the cornerstone that kept their family together, that much was clear, and it was admirable. But Eve couldn't help but wonder, was that strong, dependable exterior hiding fault lines?

And what would happen if those fault lines were pressured?

Tanner stood quietly in the middle of the lane, his hands in the pockets of his jacket. He had gloves, but he always forgot to wear them when he wasn't working. The sounds of the farm seeped into him. The cows with their soft, low voices, the horses nickering to each other as they settled in for a chilly fall night.

The chickens were long asleep with early nightfall. They'd be waking up with the sun and Devin would gather their eggs for breakfast and for selling at the farm stand tomorrow morning.

The sounds and rhythms of the ranch were as familiar to him as his own heartbeat, but even here, change was inevitable. He'd been alone here two years ago, trying not to lose the farm in a rapidly changing market. Garrett had been in town, working to get his law practice off the ground.

Then Devin returned home. A couple of months later, Lacey surprised Devin with a copy of their marriage license and a sonogram photo of the twins. Next Garrett moved home and became an unexpected daddy to a newborn baby girl named Charlotte. He brought Abby into their lives and then later married her.

With every change came challenges. Especially for Tanner, it seemed. For so long his focus had been confined to himself: to his work and his grief. Survival. Stretching beyond that was painful. Worth it to see his brothers so happy. But still not easy.

Tanner spun slowly around. Their family—and their farm—was expanding like crazy. The twinkle lights on Eve's porch glimmered through the trees. Now it seemed their family's world was expanding to include Eve and her daughter, Alice.

Lacey being out of commission was a big deal if they decided to go ahead with the Christmas party for foster families—and he didn't see how they could backtrack now. Since Eve had volunteered to help, he'd be spending a lot of time with her and little Alice. The idea made him apprehensive.

She was beautiful, confident and friendly. He wasn't much for social graces. This collaboration had the potential to be a huge disaster.

He turned back toward home. It would be fine. He would manage, because that's what he did. But sometimes he wished the Lord would let him get comfortable, just for a little while.

Chapter Three

Eve thumped a balloon into the air for Alice, who chased after it. She whacked it, and it went sailing into the air again. Hilarious laughter followed, interspersed with sharp barks from Sadie. Eve ran for the balloon again, nearly losing her balance to keep it from hitting the ground.

It was a cold, clear morning and Alice's cheeks were bright pink under her winter-white hat. Her eyes were shining, and the smile on her face made every sacrifice Eve made to get her to this point worth it.

Quit the job she loved to run a home-based business? Sure. Move to a different state to live on a ranch? No problem. There was nothing she wouldn't do to see that smile on her daughter's face.

Eve tapped the balloon again. Sadie leaped into the air to nose the balloon higher. Alice squealed, and Eve collapsed in laughter, the balloon floating softly to the ground as Alice piled on top of Eve. Sadie circled them, barking wildly.

Tanner, driving a small ATV, pulled up in front of the cottage. "Hey, neighbors."

Eve climbed to her feet, brushing dry grass and leaves off her jeans. Alice hid behind her legs. "Morning."

"Sorry to interrupt the fun." He stepped out of the ATV and reached back for a small box. "I stopped by to ask a little favor. Well, kind of a big one, actually."

"Bigger than volunteering to help with a huge Christmas party?"

He hesitated, but that slow smile started at the corner of his mouth. "Depends on how you feel about sleep."

"What's in the box, Tanner?" Eve gave him a suspicious look and crossed her arms.

In answer, he pulled back the square of fleece that covered the top of the box. Inside, curled together, were two tiny black puppies. Their eyes weren't even open yet.

"Oh, Tanner. Where did they come from?" She reached inside and picked up one of the little pups, bringing it up to her neck. When the cold air hit it, it immediately began to cry, bumping its little nose against her face.

"Devin found them in a pillowcase at the farm stand this morning. Someone dropped them off overnight. We got them warmed up and fed, and they seem to be okay."

"Oh, look, Alice. Isn't he sweet?" She crouched down so Alice could see the tiny little pup, no bigger than her two fists put together.

"I called the humane shelter, but their foster homes are all full." Tanner's voice trailed off, and she squinted up at him. The sky was bright and she couldn't see his features, only the silhouette of his leather cowboy hat.

"You want *me* to take them? I don't have any clue what to do with newborn puppies."

"It would only be until another foster home opens up. It's not hard, but I'm not gonna lie, it can be time-consuming." He reached into the box and pulled out the other puppy, cupping it in his hand. "They're pretty cute, though."

"What do you think, Alice? Think we can help these little babies for a few days since they don't have a mama? You'll have to think of names for them."

Alice nodded. She leaned forward and whispered in Eve's ear. "Daisy and Ducky."

"You want their names to be Daisy and Ducky?" Eve asked.

The little girl nodded firmly.

Eve looked up at Tanner. "Well, there you go. They have names. I guess we're on the job."

"That settles that then. Good job, Alice."

When Alice buried her face in Eve's leg again, Eve just smiled at Tanner. "You have supplies?"

"Believe it or not, we've had abandoned animals before, and I do have supplies." He handed her the box with the lone puppy, who was whining without his sibling. When she tucked the other one back in, they snuggled together and quieted down. She noted that Tanner had placed a hot water bottle in the box to keep the puppies warm.

As she took them into the house, Alice and Sadie ran in ahead of her. Tanner picked up a sack of supplies from the floor of the ATV. Inside, he placed it on the kitchen table and pulled things out one at a time. "Milk replacer. Bottles. Old blankets and towels. Baby washcloths. A heating pad, in case you don't have one."

He laid the heating pad on the table, too. "Okay, so, you mix up the milk like baby formula. Just hold their head at an angle and offer the bottle." He picked up one of the puppies to demonstrate. "They don't take much at a time, and they stop when they're full. That's all there is to it."

"That's great, thanks."

He raised one eyebrow. "Don't thank me. Garrett's usually the softy in the family. It's his fault people think we're an unofficial shelter."

"Garrett, huh? And I guess it's Garrett that's cuddling that little puppy right now?"

Tanner looked down as if he was surprised to find he was still holding it and put it back in the box with the other one. He shrugged. "It's kind of cute, I guess."

"We'll be fine. I'm excited! Plus, I know where to find you if I have questions."

He shook his head. "You better watch out. People find out about this and pretty soon you'll have baby chicks on your front porch and a piglet in your bathtub."

Eve grinned. "Wouldn't be the worst thing that ever happened. One of the reasons we chose to move to the ranch was so Alice could have the kind of childhood kids should have—with all the freedom and open air and learning about life that goes with it."

She picked up the box and moved it closer to the fire and plugged the heating pad into the wall. "When's the last time you fed them?"

"Right before I came over here. I'm not sure how old

they are—we'll know when their eyes open—but they probably need to eat every two or three hours." He cut his eyes at her. "Around the clock."

Eve winced. "*Now* I'm wondering what I got myself into."

Walking over to the fireplace, Tanner picked up the poker and stirred the embers back to life. After adding another log, he stepped back and glanced around. "Looks like Christmas threw up in here."

"Feeling a little grinchish, are we?" Eve laughed as she looked around. She had to admit that *maybe* she'd gone overboard. The amount of Christmas she'd managed to hang, tack and drape in this tiny cabin was extreme, maybe even bordering on tacky.

"Just not as into Christmas as you obviously are." With a speculative look at the collection of Santas on the mantel, he said, "I can see how it would feel perfect to a kid, though."

Glancing around for Alice, Eve saw Sadie's back end sticking out of the door to Alice's room, so she knew it was safe to talk. "Alice hasn't always been afraid of her own shadow like she is now. A few months ago, she was in the class when her preschool teacher was threatened with a gun. The guy fired a few shots. No one was hurt, but Alice was terrified. Not just by the incident—which went on way longer than it should've, by the way—but SWAT was involved in the rescue, and it was just a huge traumatic ordeal. She hasn't talked much at all since then."

"I'm so sorry, Eve. Every child deserves to feel safe." He touched her arm, just the slightest brush of his finger, but the gesture was warm, the contact comforting.

She nodded, tears springing to her eyes. She dashed them away, annoyed with herself. "Sorry. Thank you for saying that. She's gonna be okay. She's already better. It just takes time. But I think the decorations are my way of overcompensating for all she's been through."

He narrowed his eyes. "Are you trying to tell me you don't normally have Christmas spirit to spare?"

The blush was instantaneous, thanks to her fair skin. "I plead the Fifth."

He took a step toward the door. "If you feel okay with the puppies, I've got some work to do. I thought I could come back by this afternoon, maybe show you what we had in mind for the Christmas party."

"Sure, that sounds good." She walked him to the door. "I'll see you later, then."

Eve watched him as he swung into the rugged ATV and lifted a hand to say goodbye. He was such an enigma to her. She had no idea what went on in his head. Was it weird that she really wanted to find out?

She answered her own question. *Yes.* It was. He was her landlord. Her sorta friend. There were boundaries here, and that was a good thing. For both of them.

For the second time that day, Tanner knocked on the door at the cottage. When Eve opened the door, he stepped inside and took his hat off, surprised to see that she had visitors. "We can do this another time. I didn't know you had company."

"Come on in, Tanner. I want you to meet Henry and Maribeth, Alice's grandparents." She drew him farther into the room. "They've already met Sadie and the puppies."

Sadie was sprawled on the rag rug in front of the fireplace. Henry and Maribeth each had a towel over their lap and each was feeding one of the puppies.

Maribeth was a pretty fifty-something blonde with a sweet smile. She looked up at Tanner. "They are precious little things. I can't believe someone would abandon them. Whoever did it should be taken to jail."

"Can't say as I disagree with that." Henry was a little older than Maribeth and looked like the kind of man who wore khakis and a button-down on Saturday. "Tanner, glad to meet you. I'd get up to shake your hand, but I'm a little busy at the moment."

Tanner cleared his throat. "Nice to meet you both. Eve, really, our tour can wait. I don't want to interrupt your visit."

She grabbed her coat and scarf from the hook by the door. "Nope, I'm ready. Henry and Maribeth are going to babysit." Alice looked up at her mother with a scowl. "Not that you're a baby, Alice. It's just what it's called. Okay, see y'all later. I've got my phone if you need me."

Tanner followed her out the door.

She turned around, walking backward toward the ATV. "Whew. I needed to get out of there, and they need some quality time with Alice. On a different note, I think they might be willing to foster the puppies."

"What makes you say that?" He slid into the driver's seat.

"Their dog died last year, and they've been talking about getting another one. This might be just the thing for them."

"Are you always trying to fix things for people?"

She went quiet as she climbed onto the ATV beside

him, and he was pretty sure he'd stuck his foot in his mouth. One good reason not to speak without thinking first. "That wasn't a real question. It's a great idea, no matter what the reason."

"No, you asked, you should get an answer. And the answer is yes, probably, I am. I like making people happy." She stuck her hands deep into the pockets of her coat.

It was cold and breezy as they bumped along the dirt and gravel road. Tanner pulled his hat farther down on his head. "I think you're probably really good at it."

"Mmm-hmm." She flashed him a sideways look. "So tell me about the party. Is this a tradition at Triple Creek Ranch?"

"No. We had a family picnic here a couple of years ago, but this is the first time we've had the Christmas party." He turned into the drive that led to the new barn. "We figured we'd be finishing up the construction around Christmas, so it would be the perfect time for a party."

He stopped outside the large structure and slid off the seat. "We opted for a high ceiling and wide aisle. Most of the horses Devin works with are troubled. Open spaces make it easier for him to manage."

"Wow, it's really beautiful. I didn't expect this." She walked into the center of the barn, her eyes on the beams crisscrossing the pretty stained-wood ceiling. "It's beautiful."

Tanner chuckled. "We think so, but we're partial."

"No, it is." She walked around, nodding to herself. "This could really work well."

"Thoughts?"

"First impressions, really, but we could have the kids come in through that door, stand in line to see Santa and have a photo taken."

"Photo?"

"Definitely. Kids in foster care don't get real pictures of themselves very often. I could take them, but I bet we can get a photographer to donate his or her time."

Tanner nodded. He wouldn't have thought of the fact that the kids might want a photo. "I'll ask around."

"So, we can have Santa set up in this alcove here. If we really wanted to go big, we could recruit some elves to do balloon animals or face painting while the kids are waiting in line."

With a grunt, Tanner joined her in the center of the large space.

She glanced over at him. "Translation, please. Does one grunt mean yes or no?"

"Ha ha—you're hilarious. It's a great idea, I just don't know where we would find people like that on such short notice."

"Leave that to me." Eve walked down the aisle in the other direction. "So after sitting on Santa's lap, the kids walk down this aisle to wait in line for a hayride. Yes?"

"Hayrides are easy. We already have a tractor and a large trailer." Finally, something he could handle. The rest of it was making him break out in a cold sweat.

"There are some fun rental things we might think about if there's enough money in the budget. Bouncy houses and such. Kids love those, and they burn off tons of energy. I'll make a note to call around and see if anyone would give us a discount, considering it's for a good cause." Her hands were in her coat pockets again. "I'm imagining a bunch of stations—outside if the weather's nice—like frosting cookies, painting ornaments, making bags of reindeer food."

One thing was for sure—she wasn't thinking small. But he had to be honest, he was kind of into it. "What about pony rides? We don't have the kind of horses for that, but I know a couple of people who do."

Eve whirled on him. "Yes, I love that idea! This is going to be so fun."

He blinked. Her cheeks were pink from the cold, her eyes sparkling. As she did a little skip-hop dance, her scarf unwound and dipped nearly to the ground. He stepped closer. "C'm'ere."

Giving him a suspicious look, she said, "What?"

Tanner pulled her scarf—designed with reindeer faces on each end—the rest of the way off and straightened it between his hands. He looped it around her neck and tucked the ends into place so they would stay. "There."

It was an intimate gesture, and he immediately knew it had been a mistake to touch her. Her eyes were on his. Green, like the ocean on a summer day. Warm and inviting. Like Eve.

He blinked and tried a smile.

She took a step back and walked briskly to the other end of the building. "So, yeah, this is going to work great."

Tanner nodded. "The hard part is going to be reining you in."

"Oh, you do go on," she said, and he chuckled. She was irrepressible, and he liked it. He liked her.

He felt a pang somewhere in the region of his chest.

That place that always reminded him he was different, broken somehow by loss. He didn't have anything to offer to someone like Eve. But for the first time in a long time, he wished he did.

Chapter Four

Eve perched on the edge of a large chair in the Coles' living room. She was reasonably certain the painful item she was sitting on was a Lego, but finding out for sure could be awkward. She wasn't a particularly neat housekeeper, more prone to creative mess making than cleaning. Even so, her eyes widened as she took in the disaster made by the twin tornadoes named Phoebe and Eli.

Lacey blew her bangs off her forehead as a ceramic coffee mug hit the floor behind her. She didn't even flinch. "Hmm. I thought I'd moved all of those out of their reach. I gave up trying to manage the mess. When Devin and Tanner are here, they do damage control. Otherwise, it's a free-for-all."

"This stage will pass. Before you know it, they'll be in kindergarten and you'll be wishing…well, let's say you'll be nostalgic about the baby days." Eve stifled a wince as one of the diaper-clad toddlers lurched across the room to tackle Alice. She held her breath as Alice lay on the floor stunned. But then, as Alice's arms closed around the baby, a giggle bubbled out. She looked over at Eve as if to say "Mama, did you see that?"

"Alice, I think that baby likes you. Lacey, I'll be right back with the tea. Don't move," she said.

Eve ducked into the kitchen where she'd left herbal tea steeping on the counter, returning with two steaming mugs.

Lacey accepted one of them gratefully and sat back with a sigh. "This is the first time I've taken a deep breath in days. Thank you."

The Cole family's Christmas tree was wedged in the corner of the room, lit but not decorated. Eve opened her mouth to ask about it but hesitated.

Lacey raised an eyebrow. "You may as well spit out whatever you're thinking. I can see it on your face."

"Ah, I just wondered if you have plans for decorating the tree?" Caught, Eve could feel the flush rising in her face.

With a rueful smile, Lacey shook her head. "I'd planned to get everything ready inside so I could focus on prepping for the party for the kids. All the Christmas preparation got derailed when I found out I was pregnant. The guys keep saying they're gonna do it, but they're so busy during the day that I hate to ask them. They're already picking up my slack by cooking supper and putting kids to bed after a full day of work on the farm."

"May I help? It's kind of my thing, and I've run out of things to decorate in the cottage." Eve grinned. "Yesterday I caught myself wondering how Sadie would look with a red bow tied on her collar."

The dog grumbled at the sound of her name before rolling over and settling back to sleep.

Her new friend laughed. "Please, be my guest."

With Alice and Eli occupied playing with blocks on the floor and Phoebe busy careening her pretend grocery cart around the room, Eve began pulling ornaments out of boxes and hanging them on the tree.

Lacey put on some Christmas music and, for the first time since Eve and Alice had stopped by, she genuinely seemed to relax. "So, what do you do when you're not Christmas decorating? You mentioned you have experience event planning?"

Unexpected tears sprang to Eve's eyes. Impatiently, she blinked them back. She had no time for tears. She'd made her peace with her decision to leave her job a long time ago. Taking her time selecting the next ornament from the box, she willed the ache in her throat to go away. "I worked as an event planner at the Royal in Atlanta. I loved it, but the hours were nuts, and after... everything, Alice needed me more than Atlanta's brides did."

Lacey let the silence stretch, but when her eyes met Eve's, they were surprisingly warm and direct. "I know what it's like to give up a career to have a family." She waved a dismissive hand as she reached down to lift Phoebe into her lap, smiling as the little girl snuggled in for a sleepy cuddle. "Oh, I don't regret it. I don't even miss it most of the time. I stay busy with the farm stand, and it's rewarding, too, in its way."

Eve nodded. "I started a graphic design business—

T-shirts, mostly—to help make ends meet. My in-laws have offered, frequently, to let us move in with them in Mobile, but I need to make this work, you know?"

"Speaking as someone who currently lives with her brother-in-law, yes, I do."

Horrified, Eve's eyes widened. "Oh, gosh, Lacey, I didn't mean—"

Lacey laughed. "It's fine. Devin and I are building a house on the other side of the pond. One day it will be finished. But for now, it makes sense for us to be here." She tucked a pacifier into Phoebe's mouth, rocking side to side as the baby's eyes drifted closed. "I'm glad you're going to be working on the Christmas party with Tanner. He tends to hold himself back from things like that sometimes. I think it'll be good for him to be all up in the middle of it."

Eve had been steadily decorating the tree with ornaments that looked like they represented generations of Cole children. The plaster of paris handprint she picked up next had a lopsided *Tanner* carved into the bottom. It was hard to imagine stoic, manly Tanner being a child with a hand that small. As she hung it carefully on a branch out of reach of little fingers, she shot Lacey a quick smile. "I think it will be good for both of us to have a project this Christmas."

"No doubt." Lacey settled into a more comfortable position with the baby sleeping across her chest. "Do you think you could come up with a design for Triple Creek Ranch? I'd love to put some T-shirts out at the farm stand. A little free advertising for us, a few sales for you?"

"I'd love that! Thank you!"

"My pleasure. Now I'm going to see if I can get this little miss into bed without waking her up." Lacey stood, gently shushing Phoebe as she stirred.

Eve smiled. She remembered those days. There was nothing quite like the sense of accomplishment when you closed the door on the nursery, its occupant sleeping safe and sound in bed.

She picked up the last ornament, a glass cowboy boot, the shine slightly dulled with time. Eve imagined Tanner's mom lovingly hanging it on the tree when he and his brothers were little boys, fascinated by cowboys, entranced with horses and rodeos. She swallowed hard. The problem with understanding grief was that empathy could hurt. She blew out a breath, took a step back and admired the tree.

"Let me grab Eli and see if I can get him down, too. I try to keep them on the same schedule." Lacey bustled back into the room, stopping short. "Oh, Eve. The tree looks beautiful. Thank you so much. You two made my morning go by so fast, and the babies have had such fun with Alice."

She scooped Eli off the floor and was met with a resounding howl. "Can you tell Miss Alice thanks for playing with you?"

In response, Eli buried his face in his mom's shoulder and rubbed his eyes. Lacey laughed. "Okay, then, it's off to bed with you."

As Lacey left the room again, Eve said, "Want to have a race to see who can pick up the most toys? Winner gets an extra cookie at lunch!"

Alice picked up toys as fast as she could, Eve right

behind her, laughing breathlessly as they bumped into each other. "No fair, you're short. Closer to the toy box."

Alice giggled and threw another armload into the big basket next to the fireplace. She crossed her arms with an impudent smirk, her eyes full of laughter.

A few minutes later, as they were walking down the lane toward home, Alice slipped her hand into Eve's, her feet skipping every third step or so, arm swinging. And just for a brief moment, Eve caught a glimpse of her daughter before the incident, before trauma stole her voice and left her with fear.

Eve whispered a prayer of thanks, gratitude overflowing. The brief glimpse was enough, for now, to show her that the move to Alabama, to Triple Creek Ranch, had been right. Very, very right.

After a quick stop by the house to refill his coffee mug, Tanner rode out to check the animals' feed before the weather turned. The temperature was warm today, but rain was coming tonight, and after the rain, the cold would follow. That was the winter weather cycle in Alabama this time of year. *Rain, cold, warm-up, repeat. And then, just for fun, toss in some tornadoes and straight-line winds.*

When he swung Toby into the lane that would take him by the cottage, he told himself he was just going to say thanks for the casserole. Eve was on the swing outside with her tablet. Alice, as usual, was close by— on the porch steps with her crayons and coloring book, his dog at her feet.

Eve looked up with a smile. "Howdy, cowboy."

"Ma'am," he drawled, as he tipped his hat. When

Devin was on the rodeo circuit, Tanner had seen him make an entire crowd swoon with that move. Tanner just felt stupid. "What are you working on?"

She looked down, a shock of shiny dark hair falling forward over her face. When she looked up, her cheeks were pink. "Lacey asked me to draw up some T-shirt designs for Triple Creek Ranch. Maybe sell them at the farm stand?"

He stiffened slightly, feeling his control over what went on at the ranch slip once again. But it was a good idea that could benefit both Eve and the farm. "Can I see?"

She clutched the tablet to her chest for a moment, as if to shield it from his eyes, but then her grip relaxed. "Sure."

As he slid off the horse, he realized Alice's eyes were glued to the big animal. "You like him? His name is Toby."

She nodded but scooted up one step, closer to her mother. He was batting a thousand with the Fallon women today.

"He's a big guy." Tanner walked closer, leaned forward with one foot on the steps, one elbow on the rail. "He's also a real sweetheart, kind of like Sadie here."

Sadie's stub of a tail thumped wildly as she heard her name. Alice's shoulders relaxed slightly.

"He's beautiful." Eve stepped up to the rail and held the tablet out to him. "Take a look."

Tanner had a sudden fear that he wasn't going to like the designs, and then what would he say? He soon saw that he needn't have worried at all. The first design was a logo she'd created out of the *T* and *C* of Triple Creek

Ranch that had the essence of a traditional brand, a *T* perched on a *C* that encircled the *R*. It was modern and creative and… "Wow."

Her eyebrows drew together. "Wow, good? Or wow, awful?"

"Wow, good. Really good."

"Oh, I'm glad." She reached over and flicked a finger across the screen. "We can do a saying on the back, maybe like this one."

The design was simple but appealing, a circular design that said Fresh from the Farm around the top and Buy Local on the bottom. There were three beets lined up in the center. "I like this a lot."

"These are just suggestions. If you come up with something you like better, we can always change it."

He slid his finger across the screen. The next design was obviously for kids. It proclaimed in big, bold print: Future Rodeo Champ.

"I was thinking of doing these in a variety of colors. Girls and boys both could wear it."

"These are great, Eve."

"I know they're simple, but that's what I do, mostly." She hesitated. "There's one more design that's a little different than the others."

When he moved his finger across the screen this time, he brought up a clever cartoon of a tractor with a Christmas tree tied to the top of it. Lights were strung on the tree and draped across the window of the tractor. A smile tugged at his lips. "This is really cute."

"I've been playing with the design for the foster family party. I'd like to donate T-shirts for the kids."

"It's perfect. You could probably sell these or another Christmas design at the farm stand, too."

"So you're okay with me selling shirts here?"

"Yes, of course." He flipped back through. "The logo is amazing. I've wanted to do something like this, but I had no idea where to start."

"I'm so glad you like them. I've always loved to draw, but I'm new at design work and I wasn't sure if... I wasn't sure." Her voice was soft, her cheeks staining pink.

Tanner felt a stab of guilt for that foolish moment of selfishness he'd had earlier. Why was it so hard for him to reach out to others? He waited until she met his eyes before he answered her. "Putting your shirts at the farm stand makes sense. You're part of Triple Creek Ranch now."

Eve's eyes went suspiciously shiny, and he fought back the instinctive leap of fear that he might have to do something about it. He looked away, ostensibly to check on Toby, who'd made himself at home nibbling the grass along the edge of the lane.

When he looked back, thankfully, there was no sign of impending tears. He handed her the tablet. "Thanks for showing me. I'll be your first customer for a Triple Creek Ranch shirt. I've got to run. See ya, peanut. Take care of Sadie for me."

Placing his boot in one stirrup, he swung up into the saddle. He guided his horse around and clicked his tongue and they took off down the drive.

That evening, as Eve stretched a T-shirt over the press and centered the design over it, she thought of that moment. She'd stood on the step, watching him leave. Alice had tugged on her pant leg, and she'd leaned down. Barely audible, Alice had whispered, "I fink he's a real cowboy."

Eve had laughed, the tiny thread of a whisper so welcome after months of near silence. She'd swung Alice into her arms and hugged her. "I think you're right. He is a real cowboy."

Closing the press, she stepped back, stopping to rub her temple, where a headache was brewing behind her eye. Tanner was the strong, quiet, still-waters-run-deep type. A hard worker. She'd seen him heading out to work in the predawn hours and not returning until well after dark. And maybe it was silly, but she figured cowboys had a code. Some deep, intrinsic thing that made them look out for the underdog, like the cow that gets separated from the herd.

It *was* fanciful, she thought, as she lifted the top of the press and gingerly peeled the paper off the design. Way too fanciful for the reality of the man, who was just about as down-to-earth as they came, despite the fact that she'd nearly swooned as he'd swung up on that big horse.

Shaking her head, she pulled the T-shirt out of the machine and clothespinned it to the line she'd hung. Maybe she and Alice were *both* a little enamored with the handsome cowboy, which was a problem, because it could spell heartache for both of them. Tanner showed no signs of being ready to love again.

But who said *she* was ready to find love again? She'd been so busy raising Alice and working. Now, with starting her own business and trying to figure out the best way to help Alice heal, she hadn't considered it. Not really.

She didn't need to. She was fine. Single mother, businesswoman. In fact, what was she doing even thinking about this? She needed to be laser focused on making her business a success. Her ability to stay home with Alice and help her through this rough patch was dependent on it, and her funds were rapidly depleting.

She sighed. Regardless of her feelings or nonfeelings, knowing Tanner was out there made her feel safer. And safety had been hard to come by lately.

Way to go with that laser focus, Eve. She swallowed and winced, her throat scratchy. *Oh, no.* Squinting an eye toward the ceiling, she said, "Lord, you know I don't have time to be sick."

Releasing the lid on the machine, she pulled the transfer paper off the design and left the shirts to cool.

After checking the front door to make sure it was locked, she turned the lights off, leaving the night-light on over the stove. She stopped by Alice's room and tiptoed in to cover her up, smiling when she realized Sadie wasn't on the floor beside the bed but was tucked in bed beside Alice, who had one small arm draped over the thick black neck.

As Eve brushed the hair off Alice's forehead, she saw a smile flit across that sweet face. She drew in a breath, letting it go on a sigh. Progress.

The first drops of rain hit the tin roof of the cottage, and Eve shivered. She checked the thermostat, but it was a solid sixty-eight degrees. Her nagging headache was beginning to pound, but surely that was due to the coming weather change.

She wasn't getting sick. She couldn't be.

She absolutely did not have time for that.

Chapter Five

The next morning, Tanner drove the ATV workhorse around the fields of cotton they were prepping for farmers markets in the area and for sale at their own farm stand. The clouds were still spitting rain, and his breath ghosted toward the sky with every exhale.

He took out his phone to make a note that he and his brothers needed to cut the cotton and hang it to dry. Because their crop was sold for decorative purposes, they cut and dried it by hand, keeping to the organic growing practices that formed the basis of their business.

He'd had doubts when he and Garrett first considered organic farming, and the path hadn't been smooth, that's for sure. Slowly but surely, though, they'd made gains. And Devin's work with the horses had given them the room to breathe until they could turn a profit. The three of them were in the black now. Barely.

As he turned toward the back pasture, he caught a flash of pink out of the corner of his eye. Alice?

He looked closer, then drove closer, watching as the

little girl disappeared into Eve's house. She left the door cracked, not closed against the cold. Sadie appeared briefly before she, too, disappeared back into the small house.

Something just didn't seem right. Where was Eve? Should he go in and check on them? He stared at the door, willing her to come out and wave.

He was being paranoid, right? She'd been totally fine when he'd seen her the night before. Surely she was just in the back and hadn't noticed the cold air pouring in. Except that the cabin was a total of 824 square feet, and she definitely would've noticed by now.

He turned off the ATV, put one booted foot on the ground and hesitated again. So far she'd managed to keep her good nature through his unfriendly welcome, the dog moving in, Lacey on doctor's orders to rest and planning an upcoming party for two hundred people. But having him come barging into her house before breakfast? Yeah, that could be considered intrusive.

Cranking the ATV, he shook his head. He was a worrywart. Control freak. His brothers told him that all the time.

But sometimes there was something to worry about, a small voice whispered in the back of his mind.

He turned off the ATV again, and before he could change his mind, he strode up the steps to the still-open front door. He knocked and waited. There was no sound from inside except the click of his dog's toenails running back and forth on the wood floor.

Tanner closed his eyes. Sighed. What was he even doing?

Pushing the door in slightly, he called softly, "Eve?

Alice? It's Tanner. I just came by to—" What? What could he say that sounded even slightly plausible? "—check on Sadie," he finished, giving himself a mental slap upside the head. Surely he could do better than that for an excuse.

But there was still no sound from inside. His dog ran back to him, gave a woof and sat, staring at him from just inside the door. He'd seen that look before when he'd been late feeding her. She had a stare that could get a grown man to his feet in minutes. But why wouldn't Eve have fed Sadie? And where had Alice gone?

"Eve?" He pushed the door farther open. "Alice?"

The little girl's head appeared in the hall. Her blond curls were a fuzzy halo around her head. She didn't smile at him, just studied him with a serious expression. But then she crooked a finger at him.

He pointed to himself. "Me? You want me to come back there?"

She gave him a vigorous nod, her ringlets bouncing.

He closed the door behind him and took his hat off, holding it in his hands. Alice came toward him when he hesitated, waving him forward. With no sign of Eve, he was actually starting to think his worry hadn't been unfounded. When he got to the bedroom door, he found her, wrapped in a quilt and sound asleep. The TV on the dresser was streaming a kids' show, which she'd probably put on in an attempt to keep Alice occupied.

As he stood there, he saw Eve shudder and realized her skin was so pale it was almost translucent, except for two bright spots of color high on her cheeks. He crouched to Alice's level, asking quietly, "Alice, is Mama sick?"

Alice nodded.

"Okay, sweet pea, don't worry. We'll take care of her."

As she heard his voice, Eve roused and attempted to sit up. She tried to speak, swallowed hard and winced. "I'm just tired. I'm not sick."

"Obviously. Have you taken anything?" Despite his words to Alice, he couldn't help the tug of fear that something was terribly wrong. She looked awful, eyes red rimmed, lips dry.

"Couldn't find the ibuprofen." Her head dropped back against the pillow.

"I'm going back to the house to get you some. Thermometer?"

"Cabinet by the fridge." She didn't even open her eyes.

"Be right back. Alice, you stay put by Mama, okay?"

Alice nodded and climbed up to sit beside Eve, who flinched as the bed bounced. He stopped at the thermostat to turn the heat up before heading to the kitchen, that undercurrent of worry making his heart bump in his chest, goading his feet to move faster.

Eve felt someone grip her shoulder and shake her gently. She swatted the hand away. She was freezing and had finally stopped shivering.

"Eve. I have some medicine for you."

The voice was deep, a man's voice. Tanner? She opened her eyes, swallowed with a grimace and struggled into a more upright position. "Sorry," she croaked, "I kind of thought I imagined you."

He held out three ibuprofen. She unwound one flannel-clad arm from the quilt, and he dropped them into her hand. He held a glass of juice in the other hand and, after she popped the tablets into her mouth, he handed it to her, too.

"I know you have things you should be doing." Her voice was a hoarse whisper, but she managed to force the words out. "I'm really fine."

"Mmm-hmm." He pulled the temporal thermometer from his back pocket and ran it across her forehead. "One-oh-two. You're an overachiever. The doctor will be impressed."

Her mind drifted, so sleepy. His voice faded in and out, as if she was hearing him from a distance, but at those last words, her eyes popped open. "No, Tanner. Honestly. I don't need a doctor. It's probably just a cold."

"Maybe, but we're still going to the doctor."

A lot of things ran through her mind, but there was only one that really mattered. She couldn't put Alice at risk. She needed to know if she was contagious. But… "I don't have anyone to keep Alice while I go."

"She can go with us, but we'll have to take your car, because I don't have a car seat that will fit her."

"Go with *us*?"

He chuckled and took her elbow, steadying her as she got out of the bed. "Of course. You don't think I'm going to let you drive, do you?"

She closed her eyes, swayed. "I'm sorry."

"Don't be. I was going to spend the morning with the pigs in the pasture. You two are way more fun than pigs." He winked at Alice. "And smell better, too."

Alice giggled, but Eve shook her head.

"You're hilarious." She had on joggers already, so she grabbed a fuzzy sweater from the chair by the bed and clumsily pulled it on over her flannel pajama top. She was sure she looked a fright, but honestly, she just couldn't rustle up the energy to care.

Tanner left and came back into the room with a pair of pink leggings, a tulle princess skirt and a long sweatshirt. "Will this be okay for Alice?"

"Sure." Tears stung her eyes. She hated being helpless and needy. While Tanner waited outside, Eve quickly dressed Alice with shaking fingers. "Okay, baby, run on out to the living room and wait for me."

She stuck her feet in the ratty shearling knockoff boots that she wore as bedroom slippers and shuffled into the bathroom. She picked up her brush and looked in the mirror, catching an eyeful of puffy bags, too-bright eyes and bloodless lips. *Oh, this is bad.*

"Found the keys," Tanner called from the front room.

Eve sagged against the counter. What she really wanted to do was crawl back in bed and never come out.

However, on Eve's list of priorities, Alice was it. If taking care of Alice meant Eve had to act like a grown-up and haul herself to the doctor, that's what she would do. Even if it meant her handsome hunk of a neighbor saw her at her absolute worst.

Eve groaned and shuffled down the hall to the door. Sometimes being a grown-up stunk.

Tanner was waiting for her at the door. "Alice is in her seat."

"I'm ready."

"It's cold outside. You might need this." He picked up her knit cap from the hook beside the door and tugged it down over her hair. He didn't smile, just studied her with those serious eyes, and to her horror, she started to tear up. She was the one who took care of everyone, not the other way around.

"Thanks." Her voice wavered. The sore throat, obviously. She sniffed, rubbed her eyes and gathered what was left of her dignity. "Let's go."

An hour and a half later, after a quick stop at the pharmacy for an antibiotic and a run into the diner for takeout chicken noodle soup, Tanner pulled into Eve's parking spot in front of the cottage. She'd rallied a little bit at the doctor's office but was fading again now, looking like it might be a heroic feat if she made it all the way to the bedroom before she had to lie down.

She slid out of the car, and Alice climbed through the front behind her, jumping to the ground, her princess skirt floating around her. Tanner followed with Eve's meds and their lunch. She stopped at the door of the cottage. "You've been amazing. Thank you so much for making me the doctor's appointment. And for making me go."

"You should be feeling a lot better by tomorrow. I'm sorry you're sick. Strep throat is terrible."

"Yeah, don't forget the double ear infection." Her smile was wan but there.

Alice looked up at Tanner, tapping him on the hand. She whispered, "Baby pigs."

"What?" Eve looked from Tanner to Alice and back again.

"I was showing Alice a picture of the new litter of pigs that were born this week. I need to check on them."

He gave her a sheepish look. "I sort of told her she could do chores with me."

"You did?"

"Babies." Alice nodded vigorously, giving her mother a what-aren't-you-getting-about-this look with wide blue eyes.

"You're cool with this?" Eve looked back at Tanner. "For real?"

"For real. Besides, you need to rest. We can handle it, right, Alice?"

She turned pudgy little hands up with a shrug as she looked at her mom. "Baby pigs."

"I can see I'm outnumbered here. I'm going to take a nap, and you're the best, Tanner Cole."

"I have two brothers who would argue that. I've got her coat and hat." He hesitated. "Is there anything else I need to know? Allergies? Medicine?"

When he'd looked in the medicine cabinet for the thermometer, he'd found it. He'd also found a sharps container, alcohol pad and syringes. He'd stared at the collection for a long few seconds. His first thought had been that Eve could be an addict, which was a natural conclusion, he guessed, considering his brother was in ongoing recovery.

But when he'd opened the refrigerator to find the juice, he'd seen the medication, and it had Alice's name on it. *Neupogen.* A quick search on his phone had told him that the medication was used for people who had cancer to help their white blood cells recover after chemo. The same drug helped children with a certain autoimmune disease fight off illnesses that could become serious.

Eve shook her head, but her eyes stayed on her daughter. "If she gets cranky, feed her. If she gets worried or scared or isn't feeling well, bring her home."

"That's it?"

Her eyes locked with his, a hint of suspicion in them. "That's it. I'll be right here if you need me, Alice."

Alice nodded and skipped circles around Tanner. He wanted to press. Ask questions. Demand answers. But was it really his business? He knew the answer to that. It wasn't. And if he pushed, he might end up pushing her right out of his life.

Eve's face was pale, the circles under her eyes pronounced. She looked like she might pass out at any second. She reached for the door frame to steady herself.

"Do you want me to warm up some soup for you before we go?"

"No, thanks." She shook her head, but still, she hesitated.

"I'll bring her back in one piece, Eve. I promise." Because he understood her anxiety, he gently turned her around. "*Promise*. Go to sleep before you fall over."

Alice was waiting for him in the ATV. He slid in beside her. "You ready to be my farm assistant?"

She nodded, eyes shining with excitement. He had no clue why she'd decided to trust him, but he was honored that she had. He whistled for Sadie, who bounded up and launched herself into the ATV next to Alice. He turned the key and started the engine. "Before you can be my official assistant, I need to introduce you to all the animals that live here at Triple Creek Ranch. Sound okay?"

She nodded again as he turned the ATV around

and started down the lane. Mentally, he rearranged his schedule of actual farm chores. He'd be working longer hours over the next few days than he'd planned, but it was worth it. And besides, what choice did he have?

"First up, goats." He eyed her glittery pink skirt and imagined Mason or Dixon munching on the fluffy tulle, followed by wailing and tears from a certain four-year-old princess. "Er, first up, horses."

Tanner parked the ATV across from the farmhouse and waited for Alice to hop out. "This is the old barn. We're building a brand-new one, and after the big Christmas party we're having, these guys will be moving into their new house, just like you moved with your mom."

Alice turned in a slow circle, taking it in. The barn *was* old, the boards weathered, but there was something magical here. An essence of years gone by. Alice seemed to sense it, too, if the wonder in her eyes was any indication.

The back door opened, and Devin stepped inside, clapping dust off his gloves. "Where've you been? I thought you were going to come back and let the horses out to pasture." His brother's voice trailed off as he realized Tanner had company. "Well, hello."

"You might remember Eve's daughter, Alice? Eve has strep throat, so Alice is my assistant today."

Devin scowled. "Hey, no fair. I don't have a farm assistant."

Alice had backed up a couple of wary steps toward Tanner, but she smiled at Devin's silliness.

"In fact," Devin said, "why don't you and Tanner

help me lead the horses out to the round pen and put their coats on them?"

She squinted up at Tanner.

"Did you know horses wear coats?" Tanner smiled and pointed to a big gray gelding. "This horse's name is Reggie. He won lots of awards for Devin in the rodeo. You want to say hi? I can pick you up."

He waited for her to refuse, but she held her arms up. He lifted her to his hip and moved closer to Reggie, who stuck his head over the stall door so she could see him.

Devin disappeared into the tack room and came back with a handful of carrots. "Alice might want to share a few of these with Reg."

"Thanks." Tanner ran a hand down Reggie's smooth neck.

"Pretty," Alice breathed.

Reggie stuck his nose into Alice's hip, investigating. Alice leaned back, away from the huge head.

"It's okay. He won't hurt you. He's sniffing around to see if you have any treats for him."

Devin handed a carrot to Tanner, who held it out toward Reggie on a flat hand. Reggie delicately nipped it from Tanner's palm. Alice caught her breath and patted Tanner's back with her small hand, as if to say, "Good job."

Tanner smiled. She was such a little sweetheart. He held a carrot out for her to take a turn, but she put her hands behind her back, shaking her head.

"You sure? What if you put your hand over the top of mine?" He held his hand out again. Tentatively, she placed hers in it, facing up. After Devin handed them a carrot, Tanner moved it closer to Reggie, who paused to sniff the new hand before his big fuzzy lips nibbled the carrot out of her palm.

Alice's laugh spilled out in delight. Tanner and Devin shared a look. Horses and kids.

"One more?"

She nodded and, without him having to remind her, put her hand in his, so trusting. Emotion he couldn't name knotted in his chest. His habit was to try hard to be steady, to keep his equilibrium, but Alice and her mom had a way of knocking him off balance. "Okay, Reggie, this is the last one, or you'll have to go on a diet."

Alice giggled, and together they held the carrot out for the big horse. Once again, he gently took it from them and crunched it between his very large teeth.

Tanner looked down at Alice. "Okay, peanut, we need to get moving. We have a lot of farm chores to do today and Reggie needs to go outside with the other horses. First, though, I think Reggie should give Devin a kiss to thank him for the carrots. What do you think?"

The little girl nodded.

Devin gave a low chuckle and clicked his tongue at Reggie to get his attention. "Come on, Reggie. Say thanks for the carrots. Give me a kiss."

It was a trick they'd been doing for years. When Devin said *kiss*, Reggie leaned forward, lifted his nose and knocked Devin's hat off.

The antics provoked choked laughter from Alice.

"Reggie, that is not a kiss," Devin said in mock disapproval as he reseated his hat. "Be a gentleman and give me a real kiss."

Alice laughed out loud as Reggie knocked Devin's hat off again.

"I give up, Alice. He only wants my hat." Hearing the word *hat*, Reggie lengthened his neck and nuzzled Devin's cheek. Devin acted astonished, which, of course, broke Alice up even more.

One of the barn cats wove its way through Tanner's legs and Alice slid down so she could pet it. To Devin, Tanner said, "Thanks, bro. I think she fell in love."

"Aw, shucks, I'm already taken."

Tanner rolled his eyes. "I meant with the horse, you dork."

Devin laughed. "Where are y'all headed next?"

"I need to go check on Bessie's new piglets and make sure they're all holding their own. The temperature dipped pretty low last night, and it's not supposed to warm up too much today."

"Let me know if I can help. I've got a light day." Devin paused. "She gonna wear that froufrou skirt out there with the pigs?"

Tanner just shrugged. "I guess so. Why not?"

Devin was still laughing as he led Reggie out the door and into the round pen. Tanner envied his brother's ability to put the past behind him, to look ahead. It hadn't always been that way. Devin had run from the past for a long time, burying his grief in a bottle of pills. But now? His brother had found peace, or if not peace, then joy.

Mama Kitty's tail was twitching, a sure sign that she was getting annoyed with Alice's adoring attempts to love her. Tanner pushed his melancholy thoughts aside and walked to the door. "Hey, farm girl, it's time to get a move on. We've gotta go see if the chickens laid any eggs."

Alice jumped to her feet and ran to meet him, a wide smile on her sweet face, her arms stretched toward him. For a moment, he faltered, but he caught her up in his arms and walked out the door.

Being with Alice brought an ache to Tanner's chest, like a long-unused muscle waking up. It wasn't enough anymore to have the memory of his wife and child. He wanted more.

And that? Only made him feel guilty.

Chapter Six

Eve woke with a start. Her bedroom was dark, the house silent. Fear speared through her as she realized she'd let Alice go with Tanner at lunchtime and hadn't seen or heard from either of them all day. She rolled out of bed, swayed, then steadied herself.

Her throat wasn't quite as sore, and while she probably still had a fever, she didn't feel like she was going to die, so that was an improvement. Still in her fabulous outfit from earlier today, she padded down the hall to the living room, pausing when she realized that there was a fire going. She edged closer, smiling when she saw her baby girl.

Alice was sound asleep, lying on a pile of sofa cushions on the floor, a throw blanket over her. Her blond curls were a mess and she had a smear of dirt on her cheek, but she looked utterly content. One arm was wrapped around something that Eve couldn't quite see under the blanket. She tiptoed closer still. "Is that a *pig*?"

From the chair where he, too, had stretched out and fallen asleep, Tanner jerked awake. "Wha—"

Eve lowered her voice but shot Tanner a very serious mom look. "Is it possible that my daughter has fallen asleep with...an actual pig?"

Tanner grinned.

Eve took a step back. She'd never seen him smile, not like that, not full wattage. He was shockingly handsome, intensely masculine. Just...wow.

He stretched and yawned, still with the smile. "We needed to bring that little one inside because he was cold. Alice is just doing her part to keep him warm."

"I don't think my in-laws will bottle-feed a piglet."

"What? No." He laughed. "I'm glad they were able to take the puppies, but I've got this one. Truthfully, though, it's probably a good thing Alice is asleep. She got pretty attached."

"I hope she wasn't a pain," Eve said as she walked into the kitchen to make some tea.

"No—we had a blast today. How are you feeling?"

She paused. "Mmm, a little achy still, but my throat doesn't feel like it has razor blades in it anymore."

He walked toward her and leaned on the counter. "You don't sound like you feel better."

"Thanks a lot." She wrinkled her nose at him. But then her gaze caught on a crayon note propped on a bowl of farm-fresh eggs. In clumsy, childish print, it said Get Well Soon.

His eyes followed her gaze. "It was her idea. She helped me collect the eggs, and she made the card. She's pretty special."

Her throat closed up on her, tears filling her eyes. She turned away from him, busying her hands with filling the kettle, putting it on to boil.

He put his hand on her elbow, turning her toward him, his face falling as he saw her expression. "Hey, did I say something wrong?"

"Not at all. It's just, Alice *is* something special, and not everyone sees that. Her own dad—" She shook her head. "Never mind, it doesn't matter. Thank you for taking care of her today. For taking care of me."

Her voice broke, and she fought the urge to run away. Instead, she swallowed hard and looked up into his dark, serious eyes that seemed to see too much.

"Why wouldn't I take care of you?"

"No one ever has, not really." She looked away to avoid those eyes, and her gaze fell on the note again. She picked it up, brushing her fingers across the waxy crayon letters. "When I was growing up, I was the one who made the cookies and wrote the notes. My parents are nice people, but they're both doctors. They're busy with their own careers, their own lives."

"If they didn't have time for you and Alice, they're the ones who are missing out."

"I know." She wiped her eyes with the arm of her sweater. They felt hot and scratchy, and she thought she must still have a touch of fever because she surely didn't just cry in front of Tanner Cole. She picked up the kettle, pouring water in her mug as a thought took form. "Maybe that's why I love Christmas so much. It's a chance to really soak in all that childlike joy. Who doesn't love that?"

Tanner shot a look at her out of the corner of his eye. "Can't imagine."

"Stop it." She smiled up at him. "I guess I just want to create the childhood for Alice that I never had. Her little life has been hard, and she deserves all the happiness in the world."

"So do you." His voice was quiet but arresting, his hand gentle as he reached out and slid his fingers down her cheek.

Eve froze.

Tanner dropped his hand but didn't move. The moment stretched. Eve was acutely aware of the inches that separated them. The crackle of the fireplace, the wind rustling through the cotton field outside her door.

Finally, he stepped back, and the intimacy evaporated. Had she imagined it?

"You get the kid, I'll get the pig?" Tanner glanced back at her before he stepped into the living space and looked down at the pile of kid, dog and pig on the floor.

"Deal."

As Tanner deftly nipped the piglet out of Alice's arms and tucked him into the pocket between his jacket and shirt, the pig let out an incensed squeal. "I better get out of here. Sorry she's so dirty. We really did have fun."

"Thanks again, Tanner. You're a lifesaver."

"So are you, which reminds me. If you're feeling better, Lacey wants you to come to Saturday lunch. The whole family will be there, and we can talk about the party plans."

"I'll let you know."

As he closed the door with a soft snick, Eve lifted Alice into her arms. "You smell like a farm animal," she whispered, but she smiled, happy Alice had a good day.

The smile faded as she remembered that moment in the kitchen. The crackle of awareness between her and Tanner. She was pretty sure she hadn't imagined it. The real question was, did she follow up on it? He was her landlord. A friend.

No. She wasn't sure what had prompted him to touch her. It had almost certainly been completely innocent, but her heart…well, her heart wanted to believe it could be something more.

She wouldn't pursue it. She couldn't. There was too much at stake—for both of them—and she wouldn't risk her daughter's happiness to chase after something that was never hers to want.

On Friday afternoon, Tanner worked in the cotton field with his brother Devin and a crew of teenage boys they'd hired from the local high school to help. After the harvest last year, Devin had somehow dreamed up a line system made of 4x4s and buckets of cement that would move row to row with them so that they could hang the cotton stems upside down as they worked.

When the row was complete, two men would take the line from the poles into the new barn and hang it to dry. In theory, this setup was supposed to save the step of separating and hanging after harvesting. And it worked. Mostly.

With loppers in hand, Tanner paused to watch a car drive slowly down their gravel lane and turn the corner toward Eve's cottage. In-laws?

He went back to clipping and hanging—the motion repetitive and backache inducing but simple. He hadn't seen Eve in a couple of days, not since the day he'd taken her to the doctor and watched over Alice. It wasn't that he was avoiding her, exactly. And it definitely didn't have anything to do with that supercharged moment in the kitchen when he'd touched her face.

What had he even been thinking?

Ah, that. That was the problem. He hadn't thought first—he'd gone with impulse. Him, the champion of pros and cons, the one who was always saying things like *we need to think this through* or *think before you leap.* Something about Eve made him lose his composure.

He didn't like it.

As they reached the end of their row, Devin hollered to the teenage boys to come and take the lines of hanging cotton stalks to the barn. His brother had gotten some wireless earbuds for his birthday and discovered podcasts, so he was quiet today, listening to some true crime something or other. Without speaking, they moved their contraption to the next row and strung a new wire.

The car slowly drove back down the drive and, in the window, Tanner caught a glimpse of Alice's animated face as she peered out. She was a heartbreaker, that one. He knew she'd been through some traumatic things in her life. The armed gunman at her school, for one. The loss of her dad, for another.

No wonder she showed signs of traumatic stress. But in spite of it, she seemed to be thriving here. She wasn't the quiet mouse of a child who hid her face in her mother's shoulder anymore. She was cautious and watchful, yes, but she also seemed genuinely happy.

A few minutes later, Eve appeared, carrying her tablet. She had an electronic pencil in her hand and was looking up and down the road, making notations on the tablet.

He called to the boys who had finished a row and were carrying the loaded line toward the barn. "Hey, guys, take a break after you hang those. Grab a drink or a snack and meet me back here in twenty."

To Devin, he said, "Taking a lunch break."

Devin tugged an earbud from his ear and scowled. "In the middle of a row?"

"Yeah." Grabbing his bottle of water from the back of the ATV, Tanner jogged until he could drop into step beside Eve. "Hey."

"Hey, yourself. What are you up to?" Eve smiled up at Tanner. She had some color in her cheeks, and he was relieved to see that the feverish brightness in her eyes was completely gone.

"Cutting cotton. It was a big seller for us at farmers markets last year, but it's a pain to cut and dry." He nodded at her tablet. "What're you working on?"

"Right now? Just drawing out placement for some of the activities. I'm working on a master to-do list and I'm a visual learner, so the diagram helps. My in-laws got home from their trip to North Carolina late last night, so they came to pick Alice up. I'm taking the opportunity to get caught up on some work."

"Nice." He wanted to tell her she should take the opportunity to rest but restrained his impulse to cluck over her like a mother hen.

She held out the tablet to him. "I'm thinking down the lane, it would be cute to have giant candies, like candy canes or lollipops or both."

"That would be...festive." He looked down at the

tablet. She'd called it a diagram, but it was really a drawing, a talented one at that. "You have four bouncy houses sketched in over here. Can we get that many?"

She nodded. "I talked to several different companies, and once one of them committed, they all did. It's not a superbusy time of the year for them right now."

"How much is that gonna set us back?"

With a shrug, Eve gave him a smug little smile and made a zero with her thumb and forefinger. "I told them we'd put up a sign thanking them for their sponsorship."

"You're kidding. Free?"

"Well, yeah. It's great advertising for them for very little investment. There'll be tons of parents and kids here."

"Good point."

Pointing to the tablet, she said, "And down here, where they first come in from the parking area in the front pasture, there'll be a gorgeous balloon archway." She swiped the screen. "Something like this."

It was huge and bright, went with the candy theme and also looked very expensive. "Is this what we're buying with the savings from the bouncy houses?"

"Ha! Not sure yet. I'm working on that company, too. It's kind of a thing in party planning these days to have balloon sculptures." He shot her another dubious look, and she laughed. "They're cool, I promise you. Kids love 'em and parents do, too. Great pictures for the 'gram."

"The wha—"

"Instagram. You know, social media? You have an account. Or Triple Creek Ranch does, anyway." She tapped a button and went to the home page of her tablet, pressing an icon and then typing a few letters. It all took maybe ten seconds before she handed the tablet back. "See?"

He scrolled through some photos that definitely were taken at his farm. Cute baby animals. The farm stand with its bunting fluttering in the breeze. A few of Devin looking studly on a horse. There was even a picture of Tanner with one of the twins that he had no memory of taking. "Huh. It may surprise you to know this, but I am *not* on social media. This has Lacey written all over it."

"I'm not shocked." Eve took the tablet as he handed it back to her. "She does a good job. The photos are very friendly and welcoming, just like y'all are."

"People really think about this stuff?" He had enough on his plate just trying to manage his work, much less remember to take photos and put them on the internet.

"People do, yes. I have one for my T-shirt business. Here, take a look."

The T-shirts were laid out on a flat surface, mostly with jeans and bright-colored canvas tennis shoes. She'd posted a few of Alice wearing kid designs. "That looks like a lot of work."

"It is, but I'm trying to get found in a sea of people who do the same thing. Competition is stiff, and if you want to make it these days, you have to have photos people can look at." She waved an arm at the farm. "Which is why Lacey uses all this beautiful farm scenery to get people to buy what you're selling."

"Vegetables?"

Eve grinned. "Yes, vegetables. But more than that, it's the lifestyle that sparks people's imagination. And that's what we're going to do with this party. Make it so magical that the kids will never forget it."

"You're good at the magic," he said as they reached the steps to the farmhouse. "Alice's room looks beautiful with all the twinkle lights."

"Thanks, Tanner."

He cleared his throat. "Well, I definitely think we picked the right person to fill in for Lacey."

"So why do you look so skeptical?"

"It's a lot to pull off. We're going to need a lot more hands to help out." He shoved his own hands down into his pockets and rocked forward on his toes.

Eve looked down at her tablet and started typing again. "Now what?"

"Just adding it to the to-do list. *Get more hands.*"

She was joking...maybe. But the party would be here before they knew it, and both of them had a full plate already. "Bring your list to dinner Saturday. We'll get the rest of the family on board with this plan of yours."

"Sounds good. We got this. I'm going to keep walking and dreaming." She took a few backward steps toward the road. "Good luck with the cotton."

"See you later." Tanner walked into the house, not surprised to see his brother Devin, who'd beaten him in for lunch, quickly drop the curtain on one of the front windows.

Inside the living room, he waited for the smart remark from Devin. "Nothing to say?"

Devin shot a longing look across the room, where his wife was rocking Phoebe. She narrowed her eyes at him, and he sighed. "Nope."

"I'm going to make a sandwich." Tanner started for the kitchen as he heard Devin's voice.

"Except our new neighbor seems to fit in around here just fine, especially with some people."

Ignoring his brother, Tanner hid the small smile that formed. In the kitchen, Tanner's smile faded as he took in the gallery wall. Years ago, his mother had framed a recipe, special because it was in his grandmother's handwriting. When Lacey joined the family, she'd framed one of his mother's and one of Kelly's and one of her own to add to the wall. He walked over to Kelly's now, running his fingers down the glass. The recipe was written in round, loopy script.

It read: *Kelly's Famous Lasagna. Go to the store and get you a frozen lasagna. Bake it in the oven for two hours. Serve with salad. Don't tell anyone you bought it.*

The smile was back, along with an ache in his throat that never seemed to completely leave him. He'd always been the serious one, the foil to her irreverence. She'd made him laugh, and when she'd died, she'd taken his smile with her. He hadn't thought he'd ever find it again. Hadn't been sure he even wanted to.

Eve wasn't Kelly. In fact, she was nothing like her. But now he found himself smiling again. Found himself wanting to.

And he just didn't know how he was supposed to handle that.

Chapter Seven

Sitting in the driveway at her in-laws' house, Eve checked her reflection in the rearview mirror and sighed. Her mother-in-law had an uncanny ability to size up how much sleep a person got the night before, if she was eating enough, maybe even what her current temperature was. In other words, Maribeth had the mother form of spidey-sense. Eve both dreaded and aspired to that kind of intuition. Regardless, there was no fixing the haggard poststrep bags under Eve's eyes, so she might as well go in.

When the front door opened, Eve was, as usual, immediately drawn into Maribeth's embrace. For a minute, she leaned into those soft arms, letting herself rest in them.

"Sweet Eve." Her mother-in-law stepped back, placing one hand on each side of Eve's face, tilting her face so she could see her daughter-in-law clearly through the lenses of her bifocals. "Let me see you. Alice said you'd been sick."

Stepping back, Eve raised an eyebrow. "Alice said that?"

"Well, yes. I asked how you'd been doing, and she said *sick*. Are you feeling better?"

"I am. I went to the doctor and got medicine and everything. Thank you, though." She stopped, pretending to sniff the air. "Wait a minute. Are those your famous Christmas cookies I smell?"

Maribeth smiled, her blue eyes shining. "It wouldn't be Christmas without them. I loved having Alice help me decorate them this year. And before you have to ask, she did just fine last night. A little weepy at bedtime, but we turned on a show and snuggled up, and she was asleep in no time."

"I'm sure she loved being here with you. And I'm proud of her for spending the night." Eve followed Maribeth into the kitchen. With the spicy scent of apple cider and the heady scent of buttercream hanging in the air, the aroma was Christmas, and it made Eve feel happy just being here.

She dropped a kiss on Alice's head and had to laugh as Alice smiled up at her with sprinkles and a smudge of frosting stuck to her chin. Eve stuck her finger into a bowl of green buttercream and licked it. "Mmm. Can I have a spoon, please? I'm having this for supper."

Alice cackled, which woke up the two foster puppies who'd been curled into a little ball in a basket at her feet.

Eve dropped down beside them. "Oh my, look how much they've grown already. They're so cute."

Picking one up, she snuggled it close, laughing again when it yawned, its little pink tongue curling.

Maribeth looked back from the sink, where she was

rinsing some dishes. "The all-black one is Daisy, and the one with white toes is Ducky. We're going to keep them, but don't tell Henry. He doesn't know yet."

"Your secret is safe with me." Eve chuckled as she tucked the puppy in the basket next to its sibling. "Did you guys finish the Christmas tree last night?"

"Mostly." Henry appeared in the archway dividing the kitchen and family room. "We saved a box or two just for you."

She gave her father-in-law a hug, leaning in as his big arms closed around her. She loved them so. They'd chosen to accept her as part of their family when she'd married Brent. For the first time, she'd understood what that really meant.

Her parents weren't bad people, they just weren't interested. It had been their housekeeper, Alma, who'd kissed her boo-boos and helped her with her homework. And when she'd gotten married, it was Alma who'd helped her plan.

Little wonder when she'd fallen for Brent—it had been his family that had sealed the deal for her. She'd wanted them to bring her into their warm, inviting life. Of course, she hadn't imagined that her handsome, hilarious husband wouldn't always be right here beside her as they decorated the Christmas tree with his parents.

Maribeth followed them into the living room, calling back for Alice. "Honeybun, come on in here. Let's show your mom what we found last night."

"What did you find?" Eve sat on the couch with Henry on one side of her and Maribeth on the other side. Alice climbed into her grandmother's lap.

Maribeth slid a faded and timeworn box toward Eve from the middle of the coffee table. "Every year when Brent was a little boy, we collected new ornaments for the tree. Sometimes it was an ornament we bought— usually something he was into at the time, like soccer or guitar—but some of them are homemade."

Eve already had a lump rising in her throat as she lifted the top and folded back the faded tissue paper. She pulled out a soccer ball ornament and looked at Alice, her eyes wide. "Did you know your daddy played soccer when he was a little boy?"

Alice shook her head.

"Me, neither." The next ornament was a bell, made of a foam eggcup, decorated with glitter and sequins and hung by a pipe cleaner. "Oh, how sweet. I think I have one like this that Alice made."

Brent's mother smiled, but her lips trembled. "He made that one in preschool. I tried to write the dates on them so I wouldn't forget. Even back then, I hoped that one day I'd have a grandchild just like you, Alice, and that you'd want to see them."

When Alice looked up, it took Eve's breath away. With her huge smile, she was the spitting image of Brent. He'd always managed to look somewhat amused at life. Alice at her best was exactly the same way.

Eve cradled the ornament gently, her heart aching to think that Brent had made this with his own chubby three-year-old hands. Seeing these things reminded her again of the enormity of what they'd lost when he was killed. She opened her mouth to say that, but the words got stuck in her throat. Instead, she let out a strangled half laugh, half cough.

Henry put his arm around Eve as Maribeth leaned forward to speak softly to Alice. "Of course, these ornaments are very special to us, but I think your daddy would be so happy to know you have them."

Alice wrapped her little arms around her grandma as Eve cleared her throat, willing words to form. "We'll take good care of them, I promise."

Henry carefully packed the ornaments back into the old box and tied it with a ribbon. "Now, if Alice is ready to play outside, there's something we'd like to talk to you about, Eve."

Alice slid off Maribeth's lap and ran toward the back door. A few seconds later, she was climbing up the slide on the swing set her grandparents had built in their backyard for her.

Eve closed the door that had been left swinging open. "What's going on, guys? Is something wrong?"

Maribeth locked eyes with Henry, who said, "No, no, nothing like that. We just wanted to tell you we know you're working hard on growing your business, and we respect that."

Eve's fingers went still. She'd spent the night going over her finances, and the situation wasn't great. Even with Brent's death benefits, she was barely scraping by. Now this conversation was an uncomfortable reminder of how precarious her independence really was. "I'm guessing there's a *but*?"

Henry drew in a slow, thoughtful breath, and his eyes softened as he turned toward Eve. "The last thing we want is to pressure you, Eve. But if you and Alice moved in here, you wouldn't have to worry about money so much. You two could have the upstairs all to yourselves, and there's a good private school we'd be happy to pay for." He looked at his wife, who nodded her agreement. "We'd do whatever it takes to make things a little easier for you."

Eve returned to the couch, wrapped one arm around the people sitting on either side of her and pulled them in for a hug. "I love you two so much. You are just the best."

Maribeth gave her a hopeful grin. "So that's a yes?"

Eve let them go and sat back. "I love that we live close enough now for Alice to spend the night as much as she wants to. I never want to think about life without you in it. And I do need your help. I'm grateful for it."

Henry said, "Why do I hear a *but* coming on?"

She shot him a smile as he echoed her words and hesitated because she was afraid to close the door on what could be her lifeline. "But I need some time to see if I can make things work in our new place. I hope that doesn't hurt you."

Henry squeezed her shoulders. "No, sweetie. We just want you to know we're here for you. Whatever you need."

"I still miss him, you know." The words surprised her, her voice cracking. She did miss Brent, but she tried so hard not to dwell on what might have been for fear that she would miss the blessing in what was happening right now. Like raising Alice, celebrating Christmas, seeing the beauty of the farm and maybe even…well, it was too soon yet to think about the *maybes* to come.

This time it was Maribeth who nodded, tears brimming in her pretty blue eyes. "We miss him, too. And we're just so thankful we get to love the woman he loved and be a part of our granddaughter's life."

Eve sniffed and swiped away tears that clung to her lashes, laughing helplessly. "You guys, we've got to change the subject. My heart can't handle it."

"Amen to that." Maribeth bounded to her feet. "While Henry collects Alice's things, let's go get some cookies packed up for you two to take home."

Fifteen minutes later, as Eve pulled out of the driveway with Alice in the car seat and a box of cookies on the passenger seat beside her, she took a deep breath. She adored Henry and Maribeth. They'd made her a tempting offer. It would be so easy to just say yes.

So why did it feel so wrong?

Moving closer to them was a smart thing. But moving in with them would feel like admitting defeat, like she couldn't handle her life. She needed to know she could do it on her own. She'd come to the farm for Alice to heal, and she needed to keep that goal in mind. Life could be really good there.

Tanner's handsome, serious face came to mind. And not just that, she stubbornly told herself. She thought of Alice, dirt on her cheek, snuggled up with a baby pig. Yes. Her little girl was growing in confidence every single day.

But facts were facts. If her graphic design business didn't take off soon, she wouldn't have a choice. She had to make it work.

For both their sakes.

A few hours later, with the container of her mother-in-law's cookies, Eve knocked on the door of the farmhouse. She could hear a general hubbub inside, and at least one baby screaming, but no one answered the door. She looked down at Alice and whispered, "What do you think we should do?"

Alice shrugged.

"A lot of help you are." Eve knocked again, but this time she pushed the door open a crack and stuck her head in. "Hello?"

"Oh, Eve!" Entering the room from the hallway with a diaper-clad Eli, Lacey said, "Come on in. Guys, Eve's here."

A man with dark curly hair and glasses stuck his head out the door of Tanner's office. "Eve?"

When she nodded, he crossed the room and grabbed both of her hands as she juggled, and nearly dropped, the cookies. "Finally! I'm Garrett. Charlotte was teething last time we were supposed to have family lunch and honestly, it was just better not to inflict that on everyone. Otherwise I would've come to the cabin to welcome you in person."

"Garrett, let the woman come into the house." A pretty woman came in from the kitchen, her shoulder-length curls pulled back from her face with a colorful bandeau. "I'm Abby, and I'm so glad you could join us. We're having chili and corn bread—I hope that's okay."

"If I don't have to cook it, it's fine by me. This is my daughter, Alice. She's four. And we brought cookies."

"Garrett," Tanner called out from the office. "You can't just leave in the middle of the—" Tanner stepped into the living room with a scowl on his face, which brightened when he saw Eve. "Oh, hi, Eve. Glad you could make it."

Devin was next out of the office. "Guys, come on. We only have thirty minutes before lunch. Let's get this done. Hey, Eve."

Tanner crouched down beside Alice, who had her face buried in Eve's hip. He said softly, "Alice, do you want to see our favorite little piggy? He's doing great."

Little piggy? Eve saw Abby mouth the words at Garrett, who raised his eyebrows with a shrug.

As Alice followed Tanner out of the room, Garrett turned to Devin. "Weren't we in the middle of…"

Devin made a face. "Don't ask me. He left me in the cotton field with half a row picked the other day."

Eve blushed. Tanner had left Devin in the cotton field to take a walk with her.

"Weird." Garrett stared suspiciously at the door where Tanner had disappeared with Alice. "All right, well, I guess we can go over the paperwork without him."

Eve turned to Abby as the two brothers went back into the office, her cheeks burning. "When I was sick the other day, they rescued the runt of the new litter and brought him inside to make sure he was getting enough to eat."

"They. You mean Tanner and Alice?" Abby asked.

"Yes. He was really sweet with her, and she doesn't trust very many people."

"Wow." Abby's eyebrows were at her hairline as she processed this new information. "You've probably guessed that Tanner doesn't trust that many people, either."

Somewhere in the house, a baby wailed. A timer beeped in the kitchen for the second time. Abby said,

"Oh, no—the corn bread! I was supposed to keep an eye on it!"

The baby's cries grew louder.

On the other side of the room, Lacey was trying to shove Eli's arms into a long-sleeved shirt. "Eve, do you mind?"

"Shirt or crying?"

Eli popped his arm out of the shirt again and made a grab for Lacey's earring. She groaned. "Um, crying, please? It's either Charlotte or Phoebe. They're in the nursery."

Eve followed the sound of the crying down the hall. On the left were two doors. She opened the first one. Nope. Master bedroom. The next door opened into a small, bright room with two cribs. Phoebe sat in one, playing with some soft rubber blocks. She smiled at Eve around a bright pink pacifier.

The screaming was coming from the other crib. Eve leaned over the rail and picked up Charlotte. She was probably around nine months old—a redheaded, rosy-cheeked baby in ruffled purple pants and a matching lavender shirt.

"Hey, baby girl, what's going on? Were you worried when you woke up?" She felt the diaper and realized Charlotte definitely needed a change. "Or maybe you were just mad when you woke up wet."

Laying Charlotte on the changing table, she laughed at the skeptical expression on the baby's face. "It's okay, I think I remember how to do this. No promises, though."

Within a few minutes, she had Charlotte clean and dry and had managed to make her smile by making silly faces. When she turned around, she realized Tanner was leaning against the door watching her.

She smiled and shrugged, handing him the baby. "What can I say? My talents are multifaceted."

"Impressive."

Lifting Phoebe out of the bed, she said, "My next customer."

Tanner sat Charlotte on the floor beside Alice and pulled a basket of baby toys closer. A minute later, he was lying beside them, propped on one elbow, rolling a ball with the two girls. Eve had grown to know Tanner fairly well over the last week, but he still surprised her.

She stood Phoebe on the changing table and tugged her top into place. "All set, girlfriend."

"Ball," Phoebe said, as Eve set her on the floor.

"You want this?" Tanner held it up and drilled it into her stomach as she giggled. Alice was next, belly laughing as the ball drilled into her stomach, as well.

Eve couldn't help but laugh at her daughter's gleeful response. This week had been rough. She'd been on edge waiting for Alice to show signs of being sick. The worry of her finances, then having to have that hard conversation with her in-laws. But watching Alice respond like a normal little girl? That was worth every minute of hard.

Garrett appeared in the doorway. "Is it possible that someone has finally broken through Tanner's famous armor?"

Tanner's smile instantly disappeared.

Eve felt her face go hot. Garrett was making a big deal out of nothing. "Charlotte has a clean diaper. I'm going to see if I can help in the kitchen."

Eve pushed past Garrett into the hall. What she really wanted to do was run as fast as she could, back to her little house with its cheerful, superextra Christmas display and peace and quiet. After this morning with her in-laws, she'd just about had it. She pressed her fingers to her temples. Her head was pounding.

But she took a deep breath. Garrett might be irritating, but he was clearly joking. And she might be frustrated, but all she had to do was get through lunch without punching someone.

Surely she could do that.

"Devin, did you know that when Eve had strep throat the other day, Tanner took her to the doctor and then kept Alice for the whole afternoon so Eve could rest?" Garrett was going for an innocent look and missed, widely.

Tanner refrained from rolling his eyes, but just. God save him from annoying siblings. He caught a glimpse of Eve's clenched jaw. If her expression was any indication, Garrett was lucky he was too far across the table for her to punch him.

Devin looked up from his plate of mostly corn bread with a little side of chili. He sent Alice a lopsided smile. "I did know that, because I was mad Tanner got such an awesome farm assistant and I had to put the horses' coats on all by myself."

Alice giggled.

"Are you feeling better, Eve?" This from Abby, who held a sleeping Charlotte on her shoulder.

"I am, thanks. It was nice of Tanner to help me when

I was sick, especially since I didn't know a local doctor to call."

"You and Tanner should take Alice to the kids' museum in Mobile. It's really a fun place. Charlotte is way too young to enjoy it, but Garrett and I got passes anyway because we love it so much." Abby leaned forward to take a bite of her green salad.

Eve wiped Alice's mouth with a napkin. "I'm sure Tanner has enough on his plate right now."

"Is that the place Wynn had A.J.'s birthday party last month? It really is cool. Devin stayed out of trouble for an hour chasing Phoebe up and down those ramps." Lacey laughed.

"We'd be happy to babysit Alice any time so Tanner can show you around the area, Eve." Garrett nearly choked on his iced tea when Tanner kicked him under the table.

Tanner opened his mouth to say something—anything—to change the subject, but before he could get a word out, Eve put her fork down and pushed back from the table. "Lacey, thank you so much for lunch. I'm sorry we can't stay for dessert, but it's Alice's rest time."

Alice's mouth was set in a mutinous line, but Eve whisked her daughter up from the chair, hitched her up on her hip and vamoosed out the front door without another word.

Tanner leaned back in his chair and gave his siblings a disgusted look. Now what? Did he follow her? Not follow her?

Maybe he should visit her later once she'd had a chance to cool down. That seemed like the most logical approach.

"What?" Devin looked from one brother to the other, clueless, but Tanner knew things weren't right.

When someone left behind a perfectly good piece of pumpkin pie, anyone with a heart knew trouble was brewing.

Chapter Eight

It was dark outside, the moon a small sliver in the black winter sky, but Tanner knew every hole and every bump in the road that led from his farmhouse to Eve's cottage. He hefted a huge sack of dog food onto his shoulder, his excuse for stopping by. His real reason was to check on her. She'd been so quiet during lunch and had left so abruptly, he was worried that one of his knucklehead brothers had actually upset her.

When he rounded the corner toward the cottage, he saw that her twinkle lights were still on and Eve was sitting on the porch swing with a blanket, her hands wrapped around a mug. She'd dragged a small heater outside, too, but it couldn't be doing much to keep her warm.

Tanner cleared his throat so he didn't surprise her, and when he got close enough, he dropped the huge bag onto the porch with a thud. "I was thinking I'd knock on the door to check on you, but here you are."

"Here I am. Want to join?" She scooted over from the

middle and offered him one side of her blanket. Christmas songs, peaceful and instrumental, drifted out of a small Bluetooth speaker on the table beside her.

He slid into the place she'd made for him. "You were pretty quiet at lunch."

A deep sigh was her only response.

He went on. "I'm sorry Garrett was so annoying. I think now that he's married and happy, he's one of those people who wants everyone to settle down and be happy. He forgets it doesn't really work that way."

"He was being ridiculous. He doesn't know me. Didn't he stop and think maybe saying that kind of stuff was not helpful? *At all?*"

Tanner hid the smile that came with her heated words. She wasn't mad that Garrett had tried to make a big deal out of the two of them, which was what Tanner had feared. No, she was mad because she was worried Garrett had upset *him*.

"Ugh, I'm sorry. I can't even stand myself right now. I'm in such a bad mood." Eve blew her bangs off her forehead. "I was hoping some fresh air and Christmas ambience would help, but so far, no luck."

"No worries. Garrett annoys me all the time. I'm used to it." Tanner stretched his arm out across the back of the swing. "How was your visit with the in-laws?"

"It was kind of hard, actually. Emotional. Which probably explains why I couldn't deal with anything else today. I should've just skipped lunch. I'm sorry."

Tanner blinked at the rush of words, sorting through to the heart of what she was saying. "Emotional in what way?"

"They gave Alice a box of ornaments that Brent

made when he was a little boy." She picked an imaginary piece of lint off the blanket and looked off into the distance. "It was sweet."

"I can see why that would be hard, though. Do you want to talk about it?" *Say no*, he thought.

She didn't answer, the silence stretching as they rocked in the swing. Finally, her words halting, she said, "He was so full of life when I met him. I mean, he laughed literally all the time. It's what drew me to him. It's so easy to imagine him as a kid, making Christmas ornaments, being in the Christmas pageant at church making his list—all of it."

"I'm sorry. And I understand how ineffective those words really are. Firsthand."

"It's okay." When he let out a disbelieving huff, she turned toward him. "It really is okay, most of the time. If I hadn't had that time with him, I wouldn't have Alice, and Maribeth and Henry wouldn't be a part of my life. It's just…loss sneaks up on you, you know?"

His sigh was audible. "Yeah, I do know. Even after all these years, I see Kelly's handwriting or get a whiff of something that reminds me of her and I'm instantly back to that moment, knowing things'll never be the same. It still knocks my feet out from under me."

A single tear streaked down her face, and he wondered if she was reacting to his words or thinking about her husband. She stared into the darkness where the trees lined the edge of the driveway, her eyes narrowing in thought. "I think I've been living in a haze the last few years, just trying to survive minute by minute. Being here on the farm, having time to breathe— it's like coming out of a cocoon. It's painful, yeah, but

I know on the other side of the pain, I can fly. What kind of person would I be if I just stopped living because things got hard?"

She looked at him then, her eyes direct. The honesty in them sliced deep.

Still, he hesitated. Talking about his feelings wasn't exactly his strong suit. "I don't know, Eve. Sometimes I think I only went on for other people. My brothers." When he looked back, her eyes were still on him. He toed the swing into motion again. "Back then? I wasn't thankful I was alive. I was just angry that Kelly and Caleb weren't."

"And now?"

He wanted to leave, to end this conversation that was casting light into places in his heart he'd believed were better off in the dark. But he couldn't do that, not when she'd taken the risk to be open with him. His thoughts formed into faltering words. "I think living after a loss is like having a foot that's fallen asleep. Sure, it's better for it to be awake and functioning, but the waking-up process—the pins and needles—it's just so incredibly painful."

Her hand slid into his, fingers warm from the mug of tea as she tangled them with his. Palm to palm, they didn't move.

And for a moment, that cocoon seemed to envelop them, as if they were the only two people in the world. There was no today or tomorrow, or even ten minutes from now. There was only this moment with the swing rocking and Christmas music playing in the background.

Tomorrow they'd be back to real life. He'd be working on the farm, and she'd be working on her T-shirts or designing something new. They'd talk about the upcoming party, and they'd probably pretend tonight didn't happen.

And tomorrow there'd be time enough to wonder if he should feel guilty for wishing things could be different.

For wishing *he* could be different.

The next morning, Eve had just finished washing the last breakfast dish and putting it in the drainer when there was a knock at the door. She closed her eyes. *Please, don't let it be Tanner.*

Last night's conversation was too fresh. It had been good getting her thoughts out into the open. And yes, it was a blessing to have someone actually understand what she felt and not think it necessary to explain her grief away with some platitude like *things happen for a reason.* However, between yesterday's visit with Brent's parents and the disaster of a lunch with Tanner's family, she'd been left feeling raw and vulnerable.

She hated it.

The knock came again. With a sigh, Eve walked the few steps to the front door and opened it. Lacey and Abby stood on her porch, Abby holding a loaf of banana bread and Lacey, Eve's iPad.

Lacey cleared her throat. "You left your tablet at the house yesterday, so we brought it back. And...we needed to apologize."

"*I* needed to apologize," Abby corrected.

"Come on in." Eve took the loaf of banana bread and stepped aside so they could follow her into the cottage.

"I brought the banana bread as a peace offering. I'm sorry I was so…" Abby's voice trailed off.

"Obnoxious?" Lacey helpfully filled in the blank as she sat in the chair by the fire and put her feet up on the ottoman.

Abby scowled at her sister-in-law. "Well, that's not the word I was looking for, but yeah, it works. Mostly I'm sorry we made you uncomfortable, Eve."

From the kitchen, where she'd placed the bread on a cutting board, Eve shook her head but didn't bother denying it. "It's okay. I'm sure I overreacted. For what it's worth, there's nothing going on between me and Tanner."

"You didn't overreact. It's just—we all love Tanner so much, and none of us have ever seen him this lighthearted." For confirmation, Abby looked at Lacey, who nodded.

Eve slid the plate of banana bread onto the coffee table with a thunk. "This is Tanner being lighthearted?"

"Yes!"

Lacey nodded in agreement. "He really had a hard time when the twins were born. I think it reminded him too much of, you know, what happened."

Abby's eyebrows drew together under another multicolored bandeau. "It's not that he can't handle the kids. He's good with them. He just has a limit. *Had* a limit? He used to just disappear into his office a lot more."

"Yeah." Lacey nodded thoughtfully. "It's like he's slowly been coming back to life over the last year or two. Before that, it was like he wasn't there. Or he was, but not really."

"Like a foot that's fallen asleep," Eve said quietly.

"Well, yeah," Lacey said as she reached for a piece of banana bread. "Sorry. I'm starving."

What the two women were sharing about Tanner completely lined up with what he himself had said last night. Still, it was a revelation and something she needed to think about. Was he really that different with her? With Alice?

She absentmindedly bit into a slice of banana bread, then looked down at it. "This is delicious."

Abby smiled. "I'm a terrible cook. We had chili yesterday because it's the only thing Lacey lets me do by myself, and she still supervises me while I make it."

"True," Lacey said with her mouth full. "You have other talents, though."

"Yes, I do," Abby said. "Like, I'm really good at banana bread. And muffins. I can also make muffins."

Eve laughed. "Your little girl can live on muffins and banana bread. It's totally fine."

"So…apology accepted? I really am sorry."

"Apology accepted." Eve finished the piece of bread and brushed off her fingers. "Wait a minute. Where *are* the kids?"

"We hired a nanny." Lacey gave Eve a wide-eyed, can-you-believe-it stare. "The twins are so hard for me to handle alone when I'm supposed to be resting and Abby's about to be gone for ten days, so last week we talked and decided to go in together. It's a temporary solution, but for now, we both think it will really help."

"What about you? Where's Alice?" Abby asked.

"In her bedroom, having a pretend tea party with Sadie. Although there's always the possibility that she snuck actual cookies into her room."

"I can see it," Lacey said.

"So we're good?" Abby held out the plate of banana bread. "Need another piece?"

Eve laughed. "We're good. I get it—you all are protective of him. It's understandable."

"He looks tough, but underneath…" Lacey shook her head. "Yeah, we worry. And we want him to be happy."

Abby handed Eve the iPad from the table. "Now, will you show us what you've come up with for the Christmas party?"

"I can definitely do that." Her heart now several pounds lighter, Eve opened her tablet and showed them the drawings of her concept, from the balloon archway entrance to Candy Cane Lane, Sugar Plum Pasture and the Toy Workshop in the barn.

"Wow," Abby breathed. "This is fantastic."

"I've already gotten the bouncy houses and the balloon arch donated. I'm hoping the vendor I buy my blanks from for my business will donate the T-shirts for the kids. That's still to be determined."

"I love the T-shirt design with the tractor and the Christmas tree. It's perfect." Lacey was still flipping screens on the iPad. "What do you need us to do?"

"Get volunteers? Even though the crafts and cookie decorating will be simple, we're gonna need a ton of people to help."

"I can make phone calls, and I think we'll have a lot of people from church who'll want to help." Lacey made a note in her phone. "I'll ask around tonight. Speaking of which, we're having a special Hanging of the Greens service tonight at church. It's always a really nice way to start the season. You and Alice want to come?"

"I'd love to, but I don't think so." Eve wished that *yes* could be an easy answer, but it wasn't that simple. "After all she's been through, Alice still isn't comfortable with a lot of people she doesn't know. And honestly, this time of year, we try to stay away from crowds. There's always so much illness going around and Alice is especially vulnerable."

Abby looked thoughtful. "You know, working with kids who've experienced trauma is what I do. If you ever think my therapy dog, Elvis, and I could help, we'd be happy to."

"Thank you. She's doing better, but I'll keep it in mind."

Abby nodded. "Well, she has the best possible support system with a mom who's willing to do whatever it takes."

"Thank you." Eve's eyes stung at the compliment. "Moving here was a big gamble, but so far it seems to be working. She feels safe here. She's talking more and more."

"It's a great place." Lacey rose to her feet, her hands on the small swell of her belly. "I have the feeling I should get back to check and see how Mrs. Minnifield is doing with the kids. We don't want to throw her in the deep end on her first day. She may never come back."

Abby stood, too. "Eat those words, Lacey Cole. That is not an option."

Eve laughed. These sisters-in-law were a hoot. And now that she wasn't their sole focus, they were actually pretty fun to be around, too.

As they walked to the door, Abby asked Eve for some business cards. "I bought one of the Triple Creek Ranch shirts you made to sell in the farm stand, and I *love* it. I want to look at your online shop tonight and order one of your graphic designs. Then, if I have cards, when people ask where I got it, I can give them your info."

"That's so nice, thank you."

"I want the one that says Be Kind…or Else." Lacey made a fist and narrowed her eyes with a laugh as she walked out the front door.

"That one would be perfect for the social worker training event I'm about to lead." Abby turned to wave. "See ya, Eve."

"Bye, Eve." Lacey slid onto the seat of the ATV and cranked it up.

Closing the door behind them, Eve leaned on it with a sigh. That wasn't the visit she'd expected. Between her job and being a single mom to a traumatized and medically fragile kid, she hadn't had much time for friends in Atlanta. But now, with Lacey and Abby, she felt like maybe she'd just made a couple here.

She wished she could go to help decorate the church, but Alice was due for the shot that boosted her immune system, and with it being flu season—and apparently strep throat season—she couldn't risk leaving Alice vulnerable. And unfortunately, the medicine that stimulated her immune system and allowed her to fight off germs also made her body ache.

"Alice, come here, please. Time for your medicine." From the cabinet, Eve pulled out alcohol prep pads and realized the thermometer was sitting right next to the sharps container, where she disposed of the needles. There was no way Tanner had gotten out the thermometer the other day without seeing all of this. Why hadn't he said anything to her?

Alice came in with Sadie, who was wearing one of Alice's pink tulle princess skirts around her neck, following close behind. Eve lifted Alice onto one of the kitchen chairs.

"Shot time and sucker time." Eve pulled the wrapper off a sucker and handed it to Alice before washing her hands and drying them on a paper towel. They had a routine, and she tried to do the same things each time, so Alice would know what to expect.

"I bet I can do this shot in…four seconds," she said as she tore open the alcohol pad and rubbed it on Alice's tummy. "You think I can?"

Eve laughed as Alice shook her head. "You'll have to count then."

She'd done hundreds of these shots by now. The movements were rote, but the act of sticking a needle into her child, causing her pain, was anything but. Steeling herself, she pinched up the skin and quickly jabbed the needle in, slowly pressing the plunger.

Alice sucked in a breath, nodding her head as Eve counted. "One, two, three, four, and…done."

Eve pulled out the syringe and placed it on the counter while she took a princess Band-Aid she'd prepped and stuck it over the tiny spot. "All good."

Before she let Alice hop down, she gave her the medicine that seemed to help with post-injection pain. She pulled her baby girl into her arms and hugged her, rocking her slightly. "I love you. You are so brave."

Not like Eve. Eve wasn't brave at all. Because if she were being honest with herself, she'd admit that she wasn't ready to see Tanner again. She needed time to think about the conversation last night and the easy rapport she had with him, not to mention his sisters-in-law's surprising reaction to it.

She cared about Tanner—that much she would admit. Loss wasn't something you could quantify, but what he'd been through was unimaginable. The fact that he was still standing, that he still loved, that he was reaching out to her and making room for Alice, was a testament to his strength. And strength was attractive. Especially wrapped up in a drop-dead gorgeous package with a cowboy hat on top.

Yeah.

So…she could admit she liked him. Maybe he liked her, too. But she couldn't rush into anything. Or wouldn't. Because no matter what else was going on in her life, Eve had Alice to think about.

Chapter Nine

Tanner drove by the cottage on his way back to the farmhouse for a sandwich. His pigs were enjoying the mud in the wooded back pasture. With the weather warming up again and their favorite piglet getting stronger, he'd stopped by to see if Alice wanted to go with him to return him to his piggy family.

Eve was outside, painting red stripes on giant foam circles. Standing against the rail were a few she'd finished off with cellophane wrappers—they looked exactly like giant peppermints. She looked up at the sound of the ATV's engine.

"Those are great."

"Thanks. I think they turned out cute. My goal is to make thirty this afternoon, as long as Alice cooperates. My question is, where am I going to put all this until we decorate?"

Tanner had been studying one of the peppermint designs, but he looked up at her question. "You can store them in the new barn with the other stuff we've been collecting."

"Perfect. I'm expecting a big shipment of T-shirts later today, so if you don't mind, I'll store those, too."

"Of course. We're supposed to have the final inspection and get the certificate of occupancy this week, and then we can start decorating in there for real."

"I can't wait!" She did a little jig, eliciting a chuckle from Tanner.

Alice came out the front door and onto the porch, holding her shirt up around her tummy. A princess Band-Aid was hanging on by one corner. She saw Tanner and put on a sad face as she pointed to her tummy. "Boo-boo shot."

Tanner sat on the step so he would be even with her and gently tapped the bandage back into place. "You had to get a shot?"

She nodded.

"I'm sorry, farm girl. If you're up to it and Mama says it's okay, do you want to babysit Hamlet this afternoon and help feed him a bottle?"

Alice nodded vigorously, and Tanner grinned. "Okay. I've got to go eat lunch, but if it's okay with your mom, I'll come back in a little while and you can help me bring Hamlet back to his family."

"Hamlet?" Eve raised an eyebrow.

Tanner shrugged, but the corners of his mouth tugged up. "It seemed fitting, I don't know."

Twirling back into the house with her sparkly princess skirt—purple this time—floating around her, Alice was adorable. A typical kid. She didn't give any indication of being sick, but perfectly healthy children didn't get shots in the stomach.

He didn't want to be nosy. Wait. Scratch that. Yes,

he did want to be nosy. He'd been waiting for an opportunity to ask her about this since he'd seen the syringes and medicine the day Eve was sick. He lowered his voice. "Eve, does Alice have cancer? Why is she getting a shot?"

"No, she doesn't have cancer. You saw the medicine?" When he said yes, she nodded meaningfully toward the door. "She may be back and I try to make all of this as normal as possible for her, so I don't want her to catch us talking about it."

"No problem. Done." Tanner wasn't sure why he felt so panicked inside. Except he'd been through the worst possible kind of loss. He didn't let people into his life, but without even trying, he'd grown attached to these two. And the idea that something serious could be wrong with sweet Alice gutted him.

Eve picked up a stainless steel bottle of water and took a long sip. "Do you want anything? I have coffee and apple juice. And water."

"I don't want anything. Eve, talk to me. Please." He leaned one hip on the porch rail while she painted on the makeshift table she'd made out of plywood and a couple of long boards.

"Alice has what's called primary autoimmune neutropenia, which is the complicated way of saying her body doesn't make enough neutrophils, the kind of blood cells that help fight off infections. She gets the injections three times a week to help her not get sick."

"Is it—is it serious?"

When Eve stopped painting and looked at him, he could see the answer in her eyes. "It can be, just because if her counts are superlow, she can't fight off an infection. We try to minimize the risk of that. If her fever gets over 100.4, we go to the emergency room for evaluation so they can see what's going on and check her levels. I've been super on top of things this week because of my strep infection, but so far, so good."

A horrified thought crossed his mind. "Is it safe for her to be around the farm animals?"

"As long as the medicine keeps her neutrophils in the normal range, yes. She can do anything any other kid can do." She smiled at her daughter as Alice came out holding a piece of paper with a marker drawing. "Is this for me? I love the colors! Can you draw one for Mrs. Lacey's fridge, too?"

Alice flashed a smile and skipped back into the house.

He took one of the peppermint discs Eve had finished and poked at the paint to make sure it was dry. "Just wrap the stuff around it?" At her nod, he rolled out the cellophane and placed the foam circle in the center. "Are you scared all the time?"

"I used to be. When she was first diagnosed, I took her temperature four hundred times a day. Now, when I check on her before I go to bed, taking her temperature is just a routine part of it. She doesn't even know any different."

"Will she have to have shots for the rest of her life?"

Eve raised her shoulders and let them drop. "Most of the time kids outgrow this. She's had it longer than most, but she's been through a lot. We'll do a trial off the medicine when she's been stable for six months."

"What about specialists? We could go to Johns Hopkins. Or what's that one people always go to? Cleveland Clinic?"

Quietly, Eve said, "Tanner, I promise, if there were any other answer, I would've found it. She goes to one of the top pediatric hematologists in the country, at Children's of Atlanta."

He straightened and paced to the other side of the porch. Why was this so hard for him to wrap his mind around? He knew the answer—because it wasn't fair. None of this was fair for little Alice. She deserved so much better. "What can I do?"

Eve drew in a long breath. "Just be here, Tanner. There's nothing you can…fix. Sometimes that's the way things are, and all you can do is just be present."

Her face was tranquil as she painted red stripes on the disc, and he wondered at her ability to just sit with this and not be angry—although maybe that was something she'd already dealt with.

"I know, it's just—" He couldn't finish the sentence. Being present, holding space—it sounded like it should be easy, but just sitting there while a person you cared about struggled wasn't easy at all. He knew. He'd been through it with Devin's struggle with addiction.

"But Tanner, just to be clear, this is what I have to do. I'm her mother. *You* don't *have* to do anything." She didn't elaborate further.

She was trying to let him off the hook, and he grabbed at her words like a lifeline. He should be relieved, because she was right. He didn't have to do anything. And yet, that didn't sit right with him.

He crossed the porch to her, leaning forward from

the opposite side of her plywood painting table. "I don't know—I guess you two are kinda growing on me."

"Okay." She said it calmly, her eyes on his, but her bottom lip trembled. And that small tell nearly did him in.

"Thank you for telling me. I know it's probably none of my business, but I've been worried ever since I saw the sharps container and the medicine in the refrigerator."

"You care about my little girl, and that's no small thing." She put down her paintbrush and the half-painted peppermint, and before he could react, she'd wrapped her arms around his neck and laid her head on his shoulder. "Thank you."

She eased back and looked up into his eyes. This close up, he could see that she had a tiny smattering of very pale freckles across her nose and cheekbones. She was so beautiful, it made his heart ache. He closed his arms around her, brought her closer and for maybe the first time in his life didn't think before he acted. He leaned forward and brushed his lips across hers.

For a split second, she stiffened, her green eyes widening. Then she kissed him back, her mouth opening in a smile beneath his.

He kissed her again and once more. She was pure joy, heady and surprising. He stepped back and stared at her, sliding his hands down to hold hers, his mind whirling with a million wayward thoughts.

Maybe kissing her was the wrong thing to do. Maybe it was way too soon. Maybe he'd changed their relationship irrevocably. His brain was saying, *what were you thinking?* But his heart…his heart was saying, *do it again*.

"Shut up."

At first, he thought he'd said the words aloud, but no, it had been Eve who'd said them.

He blinked. "What?"

Her smile broadened. "Just stop. Shut it down. Wherever your mind is going right now, just tell it to be quiet. It's a kiss. And that's all it has to be."

His heart was still banging inside his chest, his fingers unsteady. "I've got to get back to work. For the record, I'm not running away."

She laughed as he took another step away from her. "Okay, you keep telling yourself that."

Two more steps and he was halfway to the ATV before he turned, walking backward, his eyes on her. "Hamlet and I'll stop by to pick up Alice in a little while. I'll text you when I'm on my way." He swung into the ATV. "And Eve? It might've been just a kiss, but it was some kinda kiss."

Eve tucked Alice in bed, not even pretending to shoo Sadie away when she jumped onto the bed beside the little girl. She'd given up trying to get Tanner's dog to go home days ago. The big rottweiler turned in circles, finally settling in a spot before she lifted her head and growled.

Frowning, Eve said, "I know you're protective and I like it, but if you start trying to protect her from me, we're gonna have a problem."

She reached for Sadie's head and rubbed it, but as soon as she took her hand away Sadie sniffed the air and growled again. Eve shook her head. "Okay, weird dog. Go to sleep. 'Night, Alice."

A sleepy mumble was all she got in return. She scratched Sadie one more time before retreating to the living room. Sadie might have an affinity with Alice that Eve couldn't understand, but she could be grateful that the sweet dog gave Alice confidence that she hadn't had before.

Tanner, too, had a profound impact on Alice. With her purple princess skirt flying, she'd raced out to the ATV to see the piglet she'd helped save and help Tanner release it back into the pasture with the other pigs. Yet, somehow the pig had ended up going home with Tanner again. And Alice hadn't even mentioned her legs and arms hurting tonight as Eve had washed the farm dirt off her in the bathtub.

It had been a good day. Of course, Eve had deliberately avoided thinking about the moment on the porch with Tanner. Just a kiss, she'd said to him. Not hardly.

But how could she tell him how much she was freaking out inside? She stopped at the sink and rinsed their supper plates and cups, placing them in the dishwasher. Or that she felt connected to him in a way that she couldn't understand? Kind of like her daughter and the dog, a thought which elicited a snicker.

Obviously, she couldn't tell him that. It wouldn't be fair to either of them, she thought, as she dropped a dishwashing tab into the dishwasher and turned it on.

She might be a planner, but she needed to take her own advice and just let it be. *Not* think about how his lips felt on hers. How strong and reassuring his arms

"4 for 4" MINI-SURVEY

We are prepared to **REWARD** you with 4 FREE Books and Free Gifts for completing our MINI SURVEY!

Romance

Suspense

You'll get up to...

4 FREE BOOKS & FREE GIFTS

just for participating in our Mini Survey!

Get Up To 4 Free Books!

Dear Reader,

IT'S A FACT: if you answer 4 quick questions, we'll send you 4 FREE REWARDS from each series you try!

Try **Love Inspired® Romance Larger-Print** books and fall in love with inspirational romances that take you on an uplifting journey of faith, forgiveness and hope.

Try **Love Inspired® Suspense Larger-Print** books where courage and optimism unite in stories of faith and love in the face of danger.

Or **TRY BOTH!**

I'm not kidding you. As a leading publisher of women's fiction, we value your opinions... and your time. That's why we are prepared to reward you handsomely for completing our mini-survey. In fact, we have 4 Free Rewards for you, including 2 free books and 2 free gifts from each series you try!

Thank you for participating in our survey,

Pam Powers

To get your 4 FREE REWARDS:
Complete the survey below and return the insert today to receive up to 4 FREE BOOKS and FREE GIFTS guaranteed!

"4 for 4" MINI-SURVEY

1 Is reading one of your favorite hobbies?
☐ YES ☐ NO

2 Do you prefer to read instead of watch TV?
☐ YES ☐ NO

3 Do you read newspapers and magazines?
☐ YES ☐ NO

4 Do you enjoy trying new book series with FREE BOOKS?
☐ YES ☐ NO

Please send me my Free Rewards, consisting of **2 Free Books from each series I select** and **Free Mystery Gifts**. I understand that I am under no obligation to buy anything, as explained on the back of this card.

☐ **Love Inspired® Romance Larger-Print** (122/322 IDL GQ5X)
☐ **Love Inspired® Suspense Larger-Print** (107/307 IDL GQ5X)
☐ **Try Both** (122/322 & 107/307 IDL GQ6A)

FIRST NAME

LAST NAME

ADDRESS

APT.#

CITY

STATE/PROV.

ZIP/POSTAL CODE

EMAIL ☐ Please check this box if you would like to receive newsletters and promotional emails from Harlequin Enterprises ULC and its affiliates. You can unsubscribe anytime.

LI/SLI-520-MS20

HARLEQUIN READER SERVICE—Here's how it works:

felt wrapped about her. How tender the look in his eyes was as he gazed down at her.

Or how panicked he got when his brain reengaged.

She laughed softly to herself as she sat down and looked for the Bluetooth speaker. Ah, she'd left it on the front porch this afternoon when she'd been working on the decorations. Her Christmas playlist was getting a workout this week.

Sadie beat her to the front door, scratching on the wood as Eve reached for the doorknob. "Sadie, what's your deal? Do you just need to go out?"

She followed the dog into the yard, lifting her head in much the same way Sadie did. The scent of chimney smoke on the air was cozy. Someone was enjoying sitting in front of a fire on this chilly night.

The smell was really strong, almost burning her eyes. She squinted as she looked out, peering through the trees for the porch light on the farmhouse. The air felt heavy, hazy. And she wondered, with the Cole family gone to church, were any of the neighbors even close enough for her to smell their fire?

Maybe…if the wind was right.

Sadie growled again. Uneasy, Eve grabbed a blanket off the swing, wrapped it around her and walked farther into the yard. The smell was stronger out here.

Where was it coming from?

She turned a slow circle in the yard. Did she see sparks twirling their way skyward? She glanced back at the cottage, where Alice lay sleeping and walked farther out, where she could see the closest two fields of cotton and the new barn beyond it.

Oh, dear God. The barn.

From this vantage point, she could see smoke pouring from under the roof, building and climbing, a gray smudge against a dark sky. She reached for her phone in her back pocket. It wasn't there.

Dropping the blanket, Eve ran back to the cottage, throwing open the door. Frantic now, she tried to remember where she left her phone. The last time she remembered having it was when she brushed Alice's teeth.

She ran to the bathroom and snatched it up, fingers shaking, and called 911.

When they answered, her words tumbled one over the other. "There's a fire at Triple Creek Ranch. It's at… oh, I don't even know what the address is. I'm just the tenant." She sobbed into the phone.

"It's okay, dear. I have you on the screen. I'm rolling the volunteer fire department now. Is anyone in the building?"

"No. No one's here but me. I have to go. I have to get my daughter out of danger, away from the fire."

"All right, ma'am. Help is on the way."

Eve hung up the phone and ran outside, looking in the direction of the barn. Sparks were flying higher now, too close for comfort. She had to get Alice out of here.

Back in the house, she scooped Alice up from the bed, ordered Sadie to come and ran for the front door. She grabbed her keys from a hook and opened the sliding door of the van with the remote.

She put Alice in the seat. "Sadie, load up."

The dog leaped into the back of the van, and Eve closed the door. With no idea if they'd be able to come back, she ran into the house for Alice's medicine, snatching a backpack up from the floor and shoving things in it—the thermometer, syringes, medicines.

Fear pulsed through her. She wouldn't be one of those people who ran back for something stupid and got caught in a fire. She had what she needed. At the last second, as she ran out the door, she picked up the box of ornaments and took them with her to the van.

Alice had always been one of those kids who could sleep through a hurricane. Eve was thankful she hadn't woken up. Eve put the van in gear and carefully turned it around, looking back toward the barn as she drove down the lane. Flames were shooting from the roof. Tears formed in her eyes. That beautiful barn. All the plans, all that work.

Body shaking with adrenaline, she pulled her van around to the side of the farmhouse, where they would be out of the way, but where they could see which way the fire was going. For a minute she just sat there, staring. Helpless.

The barn was burning, and there was nothing she could do to stop it. Sadie nudged Eve's elbow up and shoved her face into the tiny space she'd made. Eve scratched the big head and, with her other hand, picked up her phone and dialed Tanner's number with trembling fingers.

It went straight to voice mail. Of course he didn't have his phone on. He was in church.

She let out a shuddering breath as she heard sirens in the distance. *Please, God.* She didn't know what she was praying for, but she whispered it again. *Please.*

Chapter Ten

The Christmas tree was decorated, the church dim except for the soft glow of the lights. "Silent Night," the final hymn, drifted in a peaceful, hopeful chorus. Tanner didn't sing. He just allowed it to soak in. This service, with its familiar readings and expectant hymns, was one of his favorites of the year.

It hadn't always been that way. After his wife and baby died, Tanner had stopped going to church. He just couldn't. It wasn't so much that he'd stopped believing in God, but he'd been angry. Mad that God would allow something so awful to happen to his family, who'd done nothing to deserve it. That his brothers had to grow up without their parents who loved them so much. And that his parents would never get to have grandchildren.

It had been a dark time.

When Devin had been injured and came home from the rodeo, relying on a higher power had been part of his recovery from addiction. Lacey had joined them a few months later, and the three of them had started going together. They'd tried the big church in Red Hill Springs where he'd gone before, but it hadn't seemed to fit who they were anymore. Instead, they preferred the intimacy of the small country church near his home. Not so many curious eyes.

The church was made up of a few families, most of whom had worshipped there for generations. Older people with wizened faces who, like him, had been through things in life. They didn't ask questions. Instead, they acted as if his family had always been there. When Garrett and Abby joined them later, they were welcomed with the same easy grace.

And slowly, Sunday mornings became a tradition again in his family. His niece and nephew were baptized in that little church. It held special memories now. New memories. Some of them were bittersweet because they happened without his parents and his family, but time had softened even that grief.

The living went on living. Even when they tried not to.

Tanner took in a deep breath—replete with the smell of pine and the rich beeswax they used to polish the pews. The readings were familiar, but the wonder—that God would send his son into the world—was still there. Tanner had lost a son, and honestly, he didn't know how God could make the sacrifice.

As the voices filled the church, he found himself wishing for Eve and Alice. Eve loved Christmas so much. She would love this. And Alice would love the large nativity scene that had been placed, piece by piece, on the altar by the children of the church.

The pastor gave the blessing and invited them into

the adjoining fellowship hall for cookies and punch. A few people milled around chitchatting as they made their way to the snacks or out of the church. Tanner wasn't much for small talk, and he stood in the shadows at the back of the church, waiting for his more gregarious brothers to stop talking so he could get home.

He watched as Garrett reached for his pocket and looked at his phone, saw the look on his brother's face go from relaxed to alert. Tanner straightened.

Garrett started toward the back of the church, calling Devin to follow him. Tanner stepped into the aisle in front of them. "What's going on?"

"The barn's on fire."

"What barn?"

Garrett motioned to Abby. "Time to go."

"What's going on?" She had Charlotte in an infant car seat, hooked over her arm.

"Fire call. Barn's on fire." Garrett pulled his keys out of his pocket. "I've got to go."

Tanner grabbed his arm. "Garrett. *What barn?*"

"Our barn. The new barn. The operator said the tenant called it in."

"Eve?" Tanner's stomach flipped as he followed his brother out the door. "Is she okay?"

"I don't know anything yet. Can someone get Abby and Charlotte home?"

"I will." With Phoebe on her hip, Lacey stepped out the door of the church. "I've got an extra car seat base in the back of my van. I'll come back to the house after I drop them off."

Devin clicked open the van door and buckled Eli into his seat before taking the infant carrier from Abby and locking it into place in the rear seat. He rounded the van and kissed his wife on the head. "Be careful. I'll see you soon."

Tanner slid into the front seat of the truck. "Devin, come on."

It had probably been less than three minutes since Garrett got the message about the barn being on fire, but it may as well have been an hour. Tanner had to get home, had to find Eve and make sure she and Alice were okay. That barn was awfully close to the cottage.

And the barn. All that work. All that time and money. He couldn't think about it. Not now. He had to focus on one thing at a time.

"What happened?" Devin shot a hand through his hair. "We were about ready for the final inspection. This sets us back a year, at least."

"Let's wait and see how much damage there is. There's on fire and then there's *on fire*. Maybe it's just a little smoke damage."

They turned into the driveway at Triple Creek Ranch just as the firetrucks arrived. Tanner pulled over to let them pass. Garrett would be able to direct them where they needed to go, but they'd need little direction. In the near distance, flames were already licking the sky.

Tanner threw the truck into Park and ran toward the cottage. He had to find Eve and Alice.

Her voice stopped him. "Tanner."

He spun around, toward the farmhouse. Eve was sitting on the top step, a blanket wrapped around Alice, who was in her lap, asleep. Sadie lay on the next step down, her head on Eve's foot.

Thank You, Jesus.

Her face was streaked with tears. He sat down beside her, put his arm around the two of them and breathed for what felt like the first time in ten long minutes. "You're okay. What happened?"

"I smelled smoke just after I put Alice to bed. I walked outside and saw sparks, like a bonfire. I called the fire department, but Tanner, I think it's too late. Everything was in there. Everything for the party. All of my shirts. Your cotton. That beautiful barn."

The sinking feeling in the pit of his stomach was back. The loss of the barn was a huge blow to all he and his brothers had been trying to accomplish. "There wasn't anything you could've done to stop it by the time there were sparks. If you hadn't seen it and called it in, the cottage could've burned up, too."

He couldn't think about her and Alice being caught in the fire. Instead, he brushed the hair away from her face before he stood, stopping to unlock the door to the farmhouse. "I have to go see if I can help. Upstairs, the room on the right has two single beds. It used to be Devin and Garrett's. You two stay there tonight. Get some rest. We'll be able to tell more in the daylight."

She stood, too, shifting Alice so that her head lay on Eve's shoulder. She didn't even try to argue, just stopped in the doorway and looked back at him. "Please be careful, Tanner."

Halfway down the steps, he turned back. "I will. I promise."

Eve was awake before the sun came up. She'd heard the sound of the trucks as they left in the middle of the night, the murmur of voices downstairs and Tanner's weary, restless footsteps on the stairs as he came up to go to bed.

Alice had blessedly slept through most of the uproar, waking only briefly as Eve tucked her into bed. She'd been excited to spend the night in the small dormered bedroom that still showed signs of being inhabited by little boys.

Sadie waited by the door for Eve to let her out. She opened the door and peeked out. Tanner's bedroom door was open, the spread hastily pulled up. He'd barely slept.

She hadn't slept much, either. The terrifying second when she'd realized the barn was on fire kept playing and replaying in her mind.

Lacey looked up from her phone when Eve came in. "Morning."

"Morning. You've been up for a while." Biscuits sat on the sideboard beside a plate of ham and a jelly jar of what looked like apricot jam. The twins were in their high chairs, each with a few handfuls of cereal and some pieces of banana.

"The twins have a motto—babies don't sleep, nobody sleeps." Lacey sent her a wan smile. "Devin usually makes the biscuits, but he was so tired this morning."

"How are you feeling?"

"Not bad. I think maybe the worst is over. I'll go have some blood drawn later this week and hopefully get the all clear to get back to work. Christmas is a big season. Everyone likes fresh greenery and home-baked goodies."

"Your cookies are awesome. Tanner brought me some the first night I moved here."

Lacey brightened. "Yeah? They're a big seller at the

farm stand. I need to get back to work. We're going to need all the income we can get."

Eve looked down. She'd done some thinking about that, too, in the middle of the night. She had renter's insurance, but she wasn't sure it would cover the new stock she'd lost in the barn.

Eli threw his sippy cup on the floor, and Eve stooped to pick it up. "Have you been out there yet?"

"No. The guys will be back in soon for breakfast. Garrett told them they can't go poking around until the firefighters clear it this morning."

As Lacey spoke, the back door opened and Tanner came in, half a dozen egg cartons in his hands. He paused briefly as he saw Eve standing near the table and then continued into the room. "Morning. Alice still asleep?"

"Yes. She should be awake soon, though, and we'll get back to the cottage." She paused, not wanting to know, but wanting to, at the same time. "What's it like out there?"

"Total loss. There are some bits and pieces standing but overall, it's a burned-out shell." His eyes were rimmed with red, his hands dark with soot as he stuck dated stickers onto the egg cartons and placed them one by one into a large rectangular basket that she assumed would go out to the farm stand shortly. "Garrett's here with some kind of inspector. They asked us to clear out."

Devin came in from the front room, shaking his head. "What a mess."

"Mama?" a little voice called down the stairs.

"In here, Alice." Eve ducked past Tanner and Devin and met Alice at the bottom of the stairs, lifting her up for a hug. "Did you remember where you were when you woke up?"

Alice nodded as Eve carried her into the kitchen.

"Hungry?" Tanner smiled at Alice from the sink where he was washing his hands.

Alice nodded again, her face half-hidden in Eve's shoulder.

"Devin, if you'll grab the biscuits, we can eat breakfast." Lacey grabbed a stack of paper plates and handed them out. "We're going fancy today, people."

Abby came in wearing dress pants and a crisp white blouse, carrying Charlotte, who was asleep in the infant seat. "Hey, guys."

When the front door slammed again, Garrett came in. He grabbed a biscuit and pulled a chair in from the dining room so he could sit near the rest of them, tossing his jacket on the back of it. "Warming up out there. So. There's no evidence to support that any foul play was involved."

Tanner looked up from his plate, eyes intense, words terse. "Was that a suspicion?"

"No, but we have to rule it out in a structure fire. Looks electrical to me, but we'll see what the inspector says." His response was calmly measured as he poured a mug of coffee. "You have almond milk?"

"No, Garrett. We're farmers. We have cow milk like normal people," Devin snapped.

"Almond milk is normal for almond farmers, *Devin*."

Tanner closed his eyes, took a deep breath, and slowly opened them again. "You two are worse than the actual children in the room. Alice, do you think you could teach these boys some manners?"

Still in Eve's lap, Alice flashed Tanner a wide smile, which in turn brought a deepening of the dimple in Tanner's cheek.

Eve slowly let out the breath it seemed she'd been holding since she first saw the sparks escaping into the sky. Okay, so this was bad. It wasn't the end of the world. They were all right here, sitting around the table.

This could've been way, *way* worse.

Abby jumped up at the sound of the doorbell. "That'll be the nanny. I'll let her in, but I've got to get to work. Y'all want me to get the kids set up in the sunroom? Alice, you can come and play if you want to."

Alice glanced back at Eve, who nodded. "You can go play. I'll come and get you before I head back to our house."

As Alice left with Abby, Eve said to Garrett, "I'm assuming the cabin is okay?"

He nodded. "It's fine, no damage other than it smells like smoke. Everything smells like ash outside, though. It's hard to tell what's what."

Tanner leaned back. "So what now?"

"We get the report from the fire inspector and we get insurance to cut us a check. Then we rebuild," Devin said as he came back into the room. "Unless we can shore up our existing barn, I'm probably going to have to rent some barn space somewhere. I have new clients bringing their horses for training starting next month."

"I've got a call in to the insurance agent. I'm not sure the cotton will be covered, but maybe." Garrett took a huge bite of his biscuit. "We should know more by tonight."

Abby stuck her head back in the kitchen. "Insurance guy's here."

"What about the decorations for the party? Weren't those being stored in the barn? And, I mean, what about the party? We have two hundred people coming in less than a week. How are we going to pull this off now?" The party had not been first in anyone's mind for obvious reasons, but at Lacey's words, everyone fell silent.

"Eve? Any thoughts?" Tanner asked the question, but everyone's eyes were on her.

"All the decorations I made for the party and everything Lacey had already ordered was being stored in the barn." Eve's eyes filled. "I had seven boxes of T-shirts in the barn, too. I can't replace them, so I can't fill orders, and without that income, I don't see any way I can stay here."

"What?" Lacey gasped. "No—you have to stay."

Eve shrugged. "I have to call in to my insurance agent, too, but because the boxes were in the barn, I don't think the shirts can be covered under my rental insurance, and if your insurance doesn't cover the contents of the barn, I'm out of luck."

Tanner stood and dumped his plate in the trash can. "Nobody panic yet. We're only twelve hours into this mess. Things can and will change." His hand dropped on Eve's shoulder. "We'll figure something out."

Picking up his hat from the hook near the door, Tanner settled it in place as he walked out onto the front porch. The stench of soot and ash permeated the air, overwhelming the more familiar scents of earth and animals. It was hard to stay positive, but once again, everyone's eyes were on him. Watching to see how he reacted.

He leaned his shoulder on the post at the top of the porch steps, shoving his hands in his pockets as he squinted out at their ranch. Truthfully, he was devastated.

They'd worked too hard and risked too much to get to this point, finally able to make a profit in the coming year. He pulled his hat farther down over his eyes as his brother Devin came out the front door, the distinctive sound of his cane hitting the ground alerting Tanner to his presence.

"Stop brooding. It's gonna be all right. We've weathered worse." Devin leaned on the opposite column at the top of the stairs, watching as Garrett disappeared around the corner with the insurance agent.

"Yeah?" Tanner tipped his head to the side. "Maybe. There are a lot of unknowns right now."

Eve came out the front door, her bag over her shoulder, Alice behind her, her backpack clutched in her arms. "We're heading back to the cottage."

He nodded. "Sounds good. Thank you, Eve. If you hadn't called the fire department, things might've been even worse."

"I wish I'd noticed it earlier. I'm so sorry."

"No. There's nothing you could've done that would've prevented this." Tanner squinted, just making out a small wisp of smoke trailing upward toward winter-gray clouds.

"Dev, you ready? We need to hear what the insurance agent has to say." He sighed and pushed his weary self off the column to his feet. Garrett didn't like interference, but like it or not, the three of them were in this together. They needed to hear the verdict together.

Eve's shoulders sagged. She looked as weary as he felt, sliding her hand down the rail as she took the steps down. Alice ran ahead, her pink nightgown trailing behind her.

For longer than he wanted to think about, Tanner had felt like the lone caretaker of the ranch, of the family. And he hadn't felt like he'd done a good job at either.

They'd come so far, worked so hard to create a vision for the future of Triple Creek Ranch that they all could buy in to. He was sad and he was angry. But most of all, he was determined.

There was no other option. They would rebuild.

Devin looked up at him from the bottom of the stairs. "You coming?"

"Yeah. Right behind you."

Chapter Eleven

Despite the fact that Tanner had told her the cottage was intact, relief hit Eve smack in the chest when she rounded the corner from the lane and saw her little house sitting there, all in one piece.

The lights still sparkling on the garland that she'd looped along the porch rail drew her in, welcoming her home. She loved every inch of this ranch: the tiny cozy house, the sounds the animals made, the smell of the dirt and the plants. She was grateful for every day spent in this little piece of farm paradise.

Alice had run ahead of Eve, into the house and straight back to her room. Eve moved a little slower, taking it in. Despite the odor of smoke lingering in the air, everything seemed the same. Her eyes fell onto the little workstation she'd created out of the dining room table.

That was different. She'd known it was going to be hard to make ends meet when she moved here, but she'd held out hope every day that she was getting closer to her goal. She sat down in the hard wooden chair. It was time to be realistic. If she couldn't figure out how to turn things around, she'd have to move in with her in-laws. She took a deep breath, rubbing her forehead. She was so tired of fighting.

Brent's parents loved her and they adored Alice, but her gut told her that moving in with them and living in the shadow of her dead husband couldn't possibly be good for her or for Alice. Henry and Maribeth needed to build a life of their own. They did *and* she did.

Eve lifted her head as a squeal came from Alice's room. Was that—no. That didn't sound like Alice. She tilted her head and listened closer. The high-pitched noise came again, this time muffled but identifiable. She had a sneaking suspicion she knew exactly what she would find when she checked on Alice.

Tiptoeing down the hall, she peeked in the door, which was cracked. She could see Alice kneeling in front of the small chest of drawers but not what she was doing, so Eve tapped on the door and pushed it open. Alice slammed the drawer shut and stood in front of it.

Eve leaned on the door frame. "Whatcha doin'?"

"Nuffing." Alice's big blue eyes were wide, her gaze darting around the room, landing anywhere but Eve's face.

"What's in the drawer, Ali-Cat?"

Alice sat down in front of it and tried an innocent smile. "Nuffing."

Eve stifled a smile. "Are you telling Mama the truth?"

Alice nodded as, from inside the drawer, Eve heard

squealing that sounded, well, like a piglet that was not very happy.

"Alice Catherine Fallon, did you steal Hamlet from Mr. Tanner's house?"

"No, Mama. I wuv him." Alice pulled open the drawer, where she'd made Hamlet a very comfortable bed of fuzzy blankets and sparkly princess skirts.

Eve sighed. "We're going to have to call Mr. Tanner and see if he can come and get Hamlet, because it's going to be time for him to be fed soon."

Alice's face fell, and Eve knelt down to give her a hug, torn between laughing at the predicament and wanting to ground her four-year-old for stealing. "I know you love Hamlet, but he's not meant to be a pet or even a helper like Sadie. He's got to get healthy so he can go back to his mom and live with his brothers and sisters under the trees."

Alice drew in a long, dramatic breath and let it out. Eve gave her a kiss on the top of the head and stood. "I'm going to call Tanner and ask him to stop by when he's finished with his meeting. Hamlet can stay until then."

It wasn't until she got back into the living room and dug around in her bag for her cell phone that she realized Alice had been talking. In sentences.

She'd been waiting for this day for so long, waiting for Alice to talk to her again. And when it happened, it was a conversation about a pig. She laughed, slapping her hand over her mouth. A conversation about a pig with Alice talking as if she'd never stopped.

Closing her eyes, Eve whispered, "Thank You.

Thank You for this place and a piglet named Hamlet. Thank You for my resilient little warrior."

Remembering her phone was in the back pocket of her jeans, she pulled it out and texted Tanner.

Seeking owner of missing piglet who is the wearer of tutus and recipient of many kisses. And who would like his dad to come and pick him up ASAP.

Alice was standing frozen in the door to the hall when Eve looked up. Her face was pale, expression stricken.

"Sweetie, I know you love him, but Hamlet has to go back. We don't have what we need to take care of him here."

With tears hanging on her lashes, Alice asked, "Is Mr. Tanner gonna be mad at me?"

"Oh, baby, no." Eve picked up her sweet girl—who'd seen anger in its most destructive form—and wrapped her in a hug. "You don't have to worry that Mr. Tanner will be mad. But you do have to tell him you're sorry."

"Okay," Alice whispered, hiding her eyes in Eve's shoulder.

At the knock, Alice jumped. Eve patted her back. "Let's go open the door together."

Eve pulled open the door. Tanner stood there in his jeans and boots, looking larger than life. He must've seemed enormous to Alice. But she slid to her feet, straightening the skirt of her frilly pink nightgown. In a tiny voice, she said, "I'm sorry I took Hamlet without asking."

Tanner's eyes darted to Eve's. "Talking?"

"Yeah, that just happened."

Tanner took his hat off and stooped down to Alice's level. "Okay, so it's not cool to take people's things—er, pigs—without asking, but I'm not mad at you. I forgive you for making a mistake."

He glanced up at Eve, a question in his eyes. She nodded—his response was perfect.

Almost inaudible, Alice said, "You're not like the angry man."

Tanner's eyebrows drew together. "You mean the one at your school that your mom told me about?"

Alice took Tanner's hand and dragged him along behind her to the table, where she dug in her art box and came out with a piece of paper folded many times. She handed it to him.

"I've never seen that," Eve said softly.

Tanner unfolded the picture. On one side of the page was a small stick figure holding what looked like a very large, very black gun. The man holding the gun had a scary face with slashes for eyebrows and mouth.

Eve pressed her fist against her mouth, holding in the anguish she felt as a mother as she saw what Alice had locked inside with the words.

There was another stick figure drawn on the other side of the paper. Tanner pointed to it. "Is that your teacher? She must've been scared. I bet you were scared, too."

Alice shook her head. "Mama."

"Oh, Alice." Eve couldn't stop the tear that rolled down her cheek, but she swiped it away before Alice could see it.

"That's your mama in the picture?"

Alice nodded. "The angry man made her cry."

Tanner was silent for a long moment as he studied the picture Alice drew. Then he folded it, crease by crease, back the way she'd had it. He asked soberly, "Would you like me to keep this for you?"

When she nodded, he carefully tucked it into his back pocket and held out his hands for hers. "Alice, I want you to look at me, because this is important. I promise that no matter how mad I get at you or at Mama, I will *never* hurt you. Okay?"

She studied his face with eyes too serious for a four-year-old, but then she smiled. "Okay."

Tanner smiled back. "Now, shall we go find Sir Hamlet, faithful and loyal knight to the beautiful Princess Alice?"

With a giggle, Alice skipped back to the bedroom, Tanner following. A few minutes later, he returned with the piglet over his arm. "He was sound asleep in the middle of her drawer. You might have to do some laundry. Sorry about that."

Eve still stood by the kitchen table, her feet rooted to the floor, her heart shattered.

Tanner touched her arm. "She said she wanted to play on her tablet for a while. She and Sadie are on the bed together. Eve, she seems okay—better, even."

"Thank you."

He frowned. "So, I'm trying to piece this together. It wasn't really her teacher that was threatened?"

"No. I mean yes, there really was a domestic violence incident in her classroom, but..."

"So it wasn't you? Alice was confused?"

Eve walked to the window and looked out, fight-

ing to get her emotions under control. After all they'd
been through in the last twenty-four hours, the decorations she'd hung so lovingly and hopefully seemed
garish. Tacked on. Maybe in hopes of plastering over
the bad memories she'd moved here to leave behind. Or
maybe—if she were being kind to herself—in hopes of
making new, better memories.

She turned back to Tanner, resolute. "What Alice
drew actually happened. It was the last time she saw
her father."

"He threatened you?"

"When Brent came back from his first tour of duty,
he was messed up. He had PTSD and outbursts. It happens more than you think. I'm not making excuses for
him. It just is what it is. After that night, he left us and
went to live with his parents. And then he went back to
war." She'd always wondered if he knew he wouldn't
come back. If there was anything she could've done to
stop him. Hand to her chest, she rubbed the ache that
was always just there. "You must think I'm crazy for
talking about the ornaments and what he was like when
he was a little boy. For missing him."

Tanner shook his head. "I don't think you're crazy.
I think you're generous and loving and…amazing for
being able to see beyond the illness he had to the person underneath, the person you loved."

She studied his sincere face, sighed. "Alice was so
young, and she never mentioned it or asked about it.
How did I not know she had that memory locked away
in that little mind of hers?"

Tanner scratched his head, an impatient gesture.
"Okay, first, if she didn't show any signs of being upset

by it, how would you know? And second, I'm no psychologist or whatever, but it seems likely that what happened at her school brought up this old memory."

Eve nodded. "You're right. I have the name of a therapist who understands childhood trauma, and I've been meaning to call her. I think I need to make Alice an appointment."

"Maybe an appointment for you wouldn't hurt, either?"

She raised an eyebrow. "I will if you will."

He laughed. "I'll take it under advisement. C'm'ere."

Tanner pulled Eve into a one-armed hug, both of them laughing when the piglet squealed indignantly. He murmured against her head, "Alice is a great kid, and that's because she has such an awesome mom."

"Stop being nice to me. I'll never stop crying." Eve stepped back and laughed again through a curtain of tears. "You were perfect with her today. I can't thank you enough."

He grinned. "Well, I promised her she could feed Hamlet breakfast tomorrow, so you can thank me by bringing her up to the house at the crack of dawn."

Eve groaned as Tanner opened the door.

He looked back. "The good news of the day is that the insurance agent is going to cut us a check so we can get construction started and hopefully replace what was lost in the fire."

"That *is* good news."

"Get some rest. You look like you're about to fall over." His dimple deepened. "I'll see you in the morning?"

Tanner sat next to Alice on the porch swing at the farmhouse the following day. Alice held Hamlet in her arms while Tanner kept one hand on the pig's backside, holding him in place while he sucked down a baby bottle full of formula.

Eve sat in a chair next to the front door. The sun was barely over the horizon, but she had on sunglasses. He was reasonably certain she was asleep behind them. She hadn't moved, not even a twitch, for the past five minutes.

Devin leaned against the front door, a mug of coffee in his hand, one of the twins strapped to him in a carrier, also sound asleep.

Garrett sat on the top step, wearing work clothes instead of his lawyer getup. He hadn't said a word since he arrived fifteen minutes ago, had only poured himself a cup of coffee and joined the rest of them on the porch.

They were all feeling the strain. They'd been stretched thin already, and the fire put them all over the edge of exhaustion.

A car Tanner didn't recognize drove down the lane toward the house. "Who is that?"

"Looks like the mayor," Garrett said.

"You oughta know, considering she's your law partner." Devin's voice was dry.

A pickup truck turned in next, followed by another and another.

Wynn Grant and her husband, Latham, got out of her car. "Hey, guys."

"Morning." Tanner walked to the top of the steps as a group of men, around a dozen, clustered around Wynn. "What's all this?"

A flatbed truck full of lumber rumbled down the

lane. The mayor of Red Hill Springs grinned. "Just neighbors being neighborly, Tanner."

Tanner slowly stepped down to the ground level, flanked by Devin and Garrett. "I'm not sure I'm following."

Wynn beckoned two men forward. "James and Ezra Miller, meet Tanner, Devin and Garrett Cole."

To Tanner, she said, "James and Ezra met with me yesterday about opening a cabinetry and woodworking shop in town. Just so happens, they're also experts in barn building. They can't build your new barn back in a day—that's gonna take some time. But with Latham helping, they might be able to get your old barn spiffed up and ready for your new residents after Christmas."

Latham Grant held out a hand. "Good to see you, Tanner. Sorry about your barn. I was looking forward to seeing the finished product."

A few other guys—friends he'd grown up with—nodded their heads, murmured their agreement.

"These guys—" she hooked a thumb at them "—came to help with the farmwork and the cleanup."

Tanner was sincerely taken aback. "I really appreciate that, but y'all don't have to—"

Joe Sheehan—the chief of police for Red Hill Springs and Wynn's brother—said, "We don't have to, but I haven't forgotten how everyone stepped in to help us after the tornado messed up our house a few years back. I promised myself I'd return the favor when I had the chance. And pretty much everyone here is in the same boat I'm in."

The others nodded again. Tommy Hammond said,

"This is what neighbors do. We help each other. So you tell us what needs doing, and we'll get to it."

Devin stepped forward to shake the two men's hands as Tanner turned to Wynn, his own hands spread in front of him. "How did you pull this off? How did you even know what was going on? It's barely been a day since the fire."

"Abby," Wynn said simply. "We've been on the phone pretty much nonstop since the fire."

"And the lumber?"

She grinned. "Oh, I twisted some arms to get Masonwood to issue you a line of credit until your insurance check comes through. The Mennonite carpenters were just good timing. You don't have to do this alone, Tanner. All you have to do is say yes."

After his wife died, he'd blocked pretty much everyone out of his life. After a while, it had become a habit, so much so that he'd forgotten what real community could be like.

Tanner looked at the group of people standing around, some he'd known his whole life and some he'd never met, all who'd come together simply to help. He was overwhelmed. He couldn't get the words out over the huge lump in his throat.

"Say thank you," Devin prompted, garnering a laugh from the small group.

Tanner turned to the cluster of men standing by, waiting for his answer. "I'd be stupid to say no. Thank you. Thank you all so much for being here. Devin, if you'll show the carpentry crew where to take a look at the old barn, I'll take a few to get started feeding the cows and pigs. Garrett, do you want to show the others how to cut and hang the cotton?"

"Sure," Garrett said. "If you've got a good back, this is the job for you."

Tanner jogged up the steps to Alice and Eve, who still sat on the porch, visibly stunned. "Alice, do you mind putting Sir Hamlet back in his house?" When she nodded he held his fist out for a bump. "Thanks. You'll be around later, Eve?"

"For sure. I'll head to the grocery store as soon as it opens. I have a feeling there might be some mouths to feed." She smiled and though she was tired and emotionally drained, as they all were, he could see a twinkle of hope glimmering in her eyes.

It had been a week. But they were still standing, and together they would find a way to survive this.

It's what they did.

Chapter Twelve

Eve dumped an armload of full grocery bags onto the kitchen table. "I'm so glad your sweet nanny is letting Alice play with the babies. I bought pimento cheese, ham and peanut butter and jelly. White bread. Wheat. Small bags of chips. Sodas."

Wynn Grant, sleeves rolled up and a dish towel tucked in her jeans, closed the door to the oven. "I've just made a whole sheet pan of lunch-lady brownies, so we should have plenty of dessert, too. I don't think we've met officially. You're Eve, right?"

"Depends on what you've heard about this Eve person."

Wynn stared at her for a second, then burst out laughing. "I think you're gonna fit in just fine in this town."

Eve grinned. "Thanks. I might not be a resident for much longer, though, if I don't get some traction with my business."

Lacey looked up from laying out slices of bread. "Eve has an online store for graphic design. T-shirts and stuff. She was storing a big shipment of T-shirts in the new barn."

"Did you make the one you have on?" Wynn looked intrigued.

"Yep." Eve pulled back the flannel she'd tossed on over one of the new Triple Creek Ranch T-shirts and jeans this morning.

"You designed the logo?" When Eve nodded, Wynn said, "It's good. Let me think about it for a while. Maybe there's a way to flip this into a positive for you."

"That would be great." To Lacey, Eve said, "Do you have a big basket anywhere that I can use for chips?"

"Check the pantry–slash–laundry room–slash–pig nursery. Through that door."

Eve laughed. "I'm guessing that's Hamlet's bedroom?"

"For now. I've been trying to get Tanner to put him back in the pasture, but between you and me, he's pretty attached. Tanner to the pig, not the other way around." Lacey spread peanut butter onto the last slice of bread.

"My daughter is also very attached. If I didn't know what that pig was going to look like in six months, I feel pretty sure he'd already be sleeping under her bed."

Wynn finished washing the bowl she'd mixed up the brownies in and turned off the water. She turned back to Eve and Lacey as she picked up a dish towel and dried it. "So, Eve, last night Abby mentioned that you've been working with Lacey on the party for the foster families in our county. The decorations were being stored in the barn, too?"

"Unfortunately, yes."

"Once you figure out what you still need, let's get

together and work on it. I made a list of ladies who'd love to donate supplies and help you replace the decorations. Most of them will probably volunteer on the day of the party, too, if you need them. I know the plan was to have the party here, but since that may not be an option, I've blocked off the schedule at the park in town as a backup."

Eve gaped. "How did you manage to do all that so fast?"

"It's just a matter of knowing who to call."

Lacey raised an eyebrow. "After your years on Capitol Hill, I'm pretty sure you might know how to do a little arm twisting."

"Who, me?" Wynn gave her an innocent blink, but her ice-blue eyes twinkled with amusement. "Let's just say if I did, they'd never feel a thing."

With a laugh, Eve made an assembly line with Lacey, placing sandwiches in baggies as Lacey finished them. Wynn handed Lacey another loaf of bread and a container of bright orange spread. "Pimento cheese?"

"Sure."

"Mama?" A small voice at the door caught Eve's attention, and she turned with a smile, which faded the instant she saw the bloom in Alice's cheeks. *Oh no.*

The nanny, Mrs. Minnifield, had her hand on Alice's back. "She was playing fine up until about fifteen minutes ago, but she doesn't look like she feels well."

"Thank you so much. I'll take it from here." Eve grabbed her bag off the back of the chair and dug around in it until she found the temporal thermometer, which she ran across Alice's forehead. The monitor beeped: 103.

She looked up at her new friends. "I've got to go, guys. Alice is sick."

"Oh no, Eve," Lacey said. "Do you want some children's fever reducer?"

"I have some, thanks. She probably has strep since I just had it, but we have to get her checked out. She has an immune disorder, so she might need IV antibiotics." She found herself explaining Alice's disease for the second time in as many days.

"My brother's the pediatrician in town. I could call him for you, if you want me to," Wynn said.

Eve slid Alice's sweater on over the pajamas she still wore. "Thank you. But in this case, we have to skip the pediatrician and go straight to the hospital. It's protocol for us."

She lifted Alice into her arms, wanting to cry when she felt the hot little body against hers.

Wynn followed her to the front door, handing her a juice box for Alice. "Keep us posted, okay?"

"I will, thank you."

Tucking Alice into her car seat in the van, Eve buckled her up before pulling out fever reducer and a syringe. After Alice took the medicine, Eve handed her the juice. "Try to drink this, okay?"

Alice nodded, but her little hand was limp, and she held the juice loosely.

Pulling out of the driveway, Eve looked at Alice in the rearview mirror. "You rest, baby girl. We'll be there in a few minutes, and I bet you'll be feeling better in no time."

As she had so many times before, Eve prayed all the way to the hospital—that what she said was true, that it was a simple strep infection. And that Alice's immune system was functioning enough to fight it off.

Anything else was unthinkable.

Tanner rushed through the doors of the emergency room. He'd worked with his neighbors on the farm from early morning until the sun was starting to go down, only stopping long enough to grab a sandwich from the table Lacey and Wynn had set up outside on the porch.

It wasn't until he'd gone back to the farmhouse looking for Eve that he found out she'd taken Alice to the hospital. He'd turned right around and headed out the door before Devin had suggested maybe he should take a shower before he went to the hospital.

He'd made it from the ranch to the hospital in record time, only to get stopped at the visitors' check-in desk, where a falsely cheerful dancing Christmas tree played a song every time someone passed in front of it. All he could think about was Alice in her princess dresses, with her cheeky smile and her sincere love for a baby pig named Hamlet. At last the woman behind the desk gave him a sticker ID and directions, and he bolted down the hallway.

He pushed the door open and met Eve halfway across the room. "Eve?"

"Shhh. She's fine, just sleeping now. She does have strep, but her white count is high, which in her case is good. It means she has what she needs to fight off the infection. They're admitting her for the night for fluids and antibiotics, and when she wakes up, she's going to feel a lot better."

His shoulders sagged in relief, but his eyes were on

the tiny girl on the hospital bed, a tube taped to her hand, silvery-blond curls fanning out on the thin pillow. "I thought the last two days had been rough, but when Lacey told me you'd taken Alice to the hospital, I think I stopped breathing."

"I'm so sorry. I should've called you, but I knew you had so many things on your mind today."

"She looks so small in that bed." His voice was husky, and he cleared his throat. "She's really okay?"

"She's going to be. It's just a normal childhood illness, and she should be able to handle it. Wynn's brother, Dr. Sheehan, came by to check on her. We'll follow up with him next week to make sure the white counts are going down and stabilizing."

Tanner sank into the visitor's chair and buried his face in his hands. A second later, he felt Eve's hand on his back. "Are *you* okay?"

"I have no idea." He looked up into concerned green eyes. "It's been an unforgettable couple of days, that's for sure."

"Tell me about the farm. What's going on?"

"We got all the regular farm chores done and were able to start work on getting what's left of the barn taken down. The builders worked with Latham and came up with a plan to shore up the existing barn and add an office and two more stalls. I don't know how to put into words how grateful I am."

"It was amazing. I've always wanted to be part of a community that takes care of each other like this. It's pretty rare."

He'd been thinking about it all day, how their neighbors had shown up for them. "My mom and dad were always doing things for other people, taking casseroles over or feeding people's livestock when they had to go out of town. When I was growing up, we had a constant stream of people over to eat dinner, kids to play with, other farm families to talk about dirt and weather and cows."

She smiled. "It sounds like a nice childhood."

"It was. I didn't see it that way, after, um…after my parents died. I guess I felt like their deaths somehow negated everything that came before. Devin and Garrett didn't get that kind of childhood, that's for sure."

"The neighbors didn't rally when your parents died?"

"They did, I guess." His eyes glossed with unshed tears. "I think—I think I pushed them away."

She brushed the hair back from his face. "Oh, Tanner. You were so young and hurting so badly. You can forgive yourself for that."

"Looking back, maybe I was angry. That they were still alive and my family wasn't. I don't know. It doesn't make sense."

"It doesn't have to." Alice stirred in the bed, and Eve shushed her softly. "It's okay, baby. I'm right here."

Instantly, he was back in time, feverish and cranky. Nine years old. Maybe younger. He'd wanted to get up and go outside and play, but he was too sick. His mom's cool hand brushed across his forehead. *It's okay, baby. I'm here.*

The memory morphed into him standing beside his baby's crib in the pediatric ICU, saying the same words. *I'm right here, buddy. I won't leave you.*

He was at the door to the hall, his hand on the latch before he even realized he was moving. His chest was tight, heart hammering. "I've got to get back. Call me if you need anything."

Eve looked surprised, but she nodded. "They'll turn us loose in the morning. We'll be fine."

Her eyes were shadowed. She was exhausted, and he felt like a heel for wanting to cut and run. He clenched his jaw. Forced himself to say, "I can stay. Follow you home?"

"No. You need to get back. Tomorrow will be another long day for you, and we'll be fine." She said it again, like she wasn't just telling him. She was telling herself, too.

"I'm glad she's going to be okay." He pulled open the door and stepped out into the hall. When he looked back, Eve was sitting with her head in her hands. He wanted to go back, but he couldn't make his feet move.

He closed the door and left.

Half an hour later, when he opened the door to the farmhouse, it was dark except for the silent flicker of the television. Even the Christmas tree lights were out. The big leather chair creaked as Devin rocked one of the twins. Eli, maybe?

"How's Alice?" Devin's voice was a bare thread above a whisper, but Eli picked his head up, still awake. Devin patted the baby's back until he laid his head back down.

"She has strep, but she's going to be okay. They were giving her IV antibiotics and fluids, I think."

"They gonna admit her?"

"Yeah, just overnight. Her white cells were good—

I think that's what Eve said—so they'll hopefully be home in the morning."

"That's crazy about her immune system. Scary."

Tanner didn't say anything. He didn't have to.

"You like her, don't you?"

"Alice? Yeah, she's a sweet kid."

"You know I didn't mean Alice, so don't pretend like you don't. *Eve.* What's going on with Eve?"

"Nothing's going on." Tanner narrowed his eyes and waited. Devin had never in his life recognized the warning signs that Tanner was about to blow, and still didn't, even though they were both adults.

"You sure? You ran out of here right fast when you heard her little girl was in the hospital."

"Because she's our tenant and Alice is a sweet little girl I happen to care about." Tanner's words were measured. He wasn't going to let Devin goad him.

"Our *tenant*? Come on, Tanner, at least admit you like her."

"Fine, I *like* her, okay?" Eli lifted his head again, and Devin scowled at Tanner, who lowered his voice to a stage whisper. "I like her. But I don't know why that's any of your business."

Devin shrugged. "It's not my business, but I'm your brother and I care about you."

The wind abruptly draining out of his sails, Tanner sank into the recliner next to the one Devin was sitting in. "I'm sorry. I'm a jerk. It's just I've—I'm not even sure I know how to feel anymore. Not really."

Devin didn't judge him. He just nodded. "You numbed yourself—didn't allow yourself to think about it. I did that, too, except I used drugs to try and lock away the part of myself that could still be hurt. It made things worse, but I did it."

"I watched her brush her hand across Alice's forehead tonight, and I had this memory of Mom that was so strong. It knocked the breath out of me." Tanner didn't mention the twin memory of standing beside his son. He swallowed hard. "I just—I just don't know if I can do it again."

In the near darkness, echoing lines of grief were etched on Devin's face. "What it came down to for me was this—am I going to punish myself for my whole life for something I couldn't control? Mom and Dad wouldn't want me to be miserable, or worse, kill myself with drugs because they weren't here and I felt guilty. Even if what happened was my fault, they wouldn't want that. And maybe I'm taking some huge liberties here, but I don't think Kelly would want that for you, either."

Tanner's head jerked up, and Devin held up a hand. "That's as far as I'm going with that, but think about it. I'm the first to admit taking that step, letting other people in, is *terrifying*. And you're the only one who can decide if it's worth it."

"And how exactly do I do that?"

Devin shrugged. "Faith over fear."

Tanner snorted. "Yeah, okay."

"I said it wasn't easy, but I'm also saying if you want to find joy, that's where it lives." Eli's pacifier fell out of his mouth. Devin caught it with his free hand and stood. "He's finally asleep. I'm gonna put him down and try to get some rest before he wakes up again."

"Night." After Devin left, Tanner sat in the darkness, watching a late-night comedy show on the TV. The host was laughing, the guest making faces and moving his lips—telling a story, Tanner guessed. Without any way to know what they were saying, it all seemed so meaningless. Just like his life. He'd had this experience that he couldn't make sense of when his family died, so he'd stopped trying.

Faith over fear.

Simple truth. Leap of faith.

So why did it seem like such an impossible thing to attain?

Chapter Thirteen

Eve finally got home from the hospital with Alice a little after ten in the morning, having spent the entire ride home on the phone with her mother-in-law trying to explain why she hadn't called them when she realized Alice was sick.

Truth was, she didn't have an explanation. She'd been on her own with Alice for the better part of four years, and it just hadn't crossed her mind to call them. She turned the car off and said a small prayer of thanks that they'd made it back to the cottage. "Come on, Ali-Cat. We're finally home."

"I'm hungry. And I want a show." Alice was cranky, having been woken every hour on the hour last night to have her temperature checked by the nurses.

"Coming right up." On the way to the bedroom, Eve turned on the coffeepot. She grabbed Alice's pillow off the bed and the extra blankets from the hall linen closet and piled them on the couch. "Okay, hop in. Let's make sure you don't have a fever, and then I'll get you a snack."

"Cookies."

"Fine." Digging through her purse, Eve found the thermometer and slid it across Alice's forehead—99.6. Perfectly acceptable. Alice's temp hadn't spiked above a hundred all night. *Thank you, antibiotics.*

In the kitchen, she pulled her favorite mug out of the cabinet and pressed the button for coffee. If Alice had had fitful sleep, Eve had barely dozed. The bags under her eyes were so big she could literally see them when she was looking straight ahead.

She added a splash of half-and-half, which basically only served the purpose of cooling the coffee down enough for her to chug the first cup.

With her eyes slightly more open and the second cup of coffee cooling in her mug, she stuck a straw in a juice box for Alice and handed her a couple of oatmeal cookies. Right now oatmeal equaled breakfast food, so she was totally killing this mom thing.

Sadie jumped onto the couch beside Alice and settled in with her head on Alice's hip. Alice broke off a piece of her cookie and handed it to the dog without looking away from the television.

Eve would gladly put up with a whiny four-year-old for months on end if it meant Alice was really talking, not just saying words and phrases here and there. She'd been praying for this moment since Alice witnessed her teacher being threatened so many months ago.

That event had flipped a switch, and Eve hadn't been sure she'd ever get her happy-go-lucky little girl back. But thanks to fresh air, farm life, a big black rottie and a little fuzzy piglet—not to mention a handsome cowboy—she had.

It was something good that had happened in this awful, awful week. Exhausted and emotional, Tanner had been showing the strain last night. Eve wondered if he'd felt better when he woke up this morning or if, like Alice, he'd woken up cranky, too.

Taking her cup of coffee, she sat down in the recliner. With Alice settled on the couch, Eve thought she'd relax for a few minutes.

She jerked awake an hour later. Alice was sound asleep. Sadie, too. Eve rolled to her feet, took Alice's temperature again and breathed a sigh of relief, just like she did every single time the thermometer reading was normal.

Grabbing a granola bar out of the snack bowl she kept on the counter, she walked outside. The ladder she'd borrowed from the shed to clean out the gutter along the front edge of the roof was still leaning against the side of the house. That would have to wait for another day.

She heard Tanner before she saw him turn the corner and trot up on his horse. "Hey, I thought I heard you drive in a while ago. How's Alice feeling?"

"She's sleeping now, but her temperature's normal."

Tanner's smile echoed her own. "Best news I've heard all day."

"How are things going with the cleanup?"

His horse shimmied a little to the right, and Tanner tightened the reins. "Simmer down, Toby. It's a little tough to think about how close we were to having the new barn ready to use, but we're trying to focus on how to keep moving forward."

Eve would love to focus on moving forward, but

truthfully there was no way for her to afford new shirts, not now. She'd sent a message to everyone who'd ordered and readjusted the delivery date with her apologies. But unless she got insurance money, she wasn't sure how she could buy more T-shirts to fulfill the orders. And sending money back that she didn't have wasn't an option, either. She forced a smile. "One step at a time."

"Right." Tanner spoke again in a low, deep voice to the horse, which seemed like a bundle of muscle about to explode, then said, "Do you think Alice would be up to visiting the church tonight? I asked the pastor, and he said he wouldn't mind if we take a private tour since she can't be around crowds."

"I think she'd love an outing. I should warn you, though, she was a wee bit demanding this morning."

"I don't mind." He turned the horse in a small circle. "Toby is a little demanding this morning, too. He hasn't been ridden enough, and he's itching for me to give him his head. Pick you up around dark?"

"Sure."

Tanner pushed his hat farther down on his head and turned Toby toward the road. Eve could see he had a little trouble keeping the energetic horse to a walk but had no problem at all accelerating when they reached the lane.

She ran a hand through her hair and sighed. No, she wasn't focused on moving on. She was focused on survival. It was hard not to feel bitter that everything she'd worked toward was at risk. However, despite the dismal state of her bank account, Alice was doing well—

better every day—and Eve would trade every dime she had to see that.

Positive self-talk refilled the tank, or so her counselor had told her after Brent died. If only she could refill her bank account as easily.

Tanner glanced back at Eve and Alice as they followed him up the walkway to the white clapboard church. A soft glow came from the simple stained glass windows.

He used his key to open the front door, which was painted a glossy red. "When I first started coming here, I thought the red door seemed weird for a little country church, so I did some reading up. Apparently, it's a tradition from the Middle Ages and was a sign that you could find refuge behind those doors. Kind of fitting, if you ask me."

Eve's eyes lingered on the live greenery hung on the doors, the scent of the cedar giving the air a heady evergreen fragrance as they walked into the sanctuary.

She stopped just inside the door, her breath catching in her throat. "It's so beautiful."

The church had been built almost two hundred years ago and still had the same dark wood interior, carved by talented craftsmen. Each window had been dressed with greenery and a globe with a candle.

A real Christmas tree was on each side of the altar, covered with beaded ornaments of white and gold that had been painstakingly made over the years by the women in the church. But to him, the most beautiful thing about the way they decorated this church was the lights they hung from the high, high ceiling. Hundreds of twinkle lights dangled from the wide beams.

Eve looked up in awe. "It feels like looking into a dark sky full of stars. It makes you feel so small."

"It's supposed to feel like you're one of the shepherds or the wise men watching the sky for signs. Or at least, that's what I'm told."

Alice wandered up to the altar, where a large nativity scene had been set. She reached out a hand and touched the carved blue drape of Mary's robe with a tentative finger.

"Alice, don't touch, please."

The little girl pulled her hand back, but she said, "Where's the baby Jesus? You can't have Christmas without the baby."

Tanner smiled as he walked up to stand beside her. "You're right, you can't. We have a tradition in this church. On the night we decorate, all the Bible verses are read about all the people who helped celebrate Jesus being born, and all of the nativity figures are put in place by the children of the church. On Christmas Eve, during the children's message, they'll put the baby in the manger."

Without looking at him, Alice slid her small hand into his, and he melted. He closed his eyes and said a prayer that he would be worthy of the trust of this sweet, careful child.

Eve was sitting in the pew in the back of the church, leaning back so she could get the whole ceiling in her view. He eased in beside her as Alice explored along the altar rail. "You okay?"

She nodded but then shook her head.

"What's wrong? Can I help?"

"I'm thankful that you care about Alice. She has her grandpa, but it's really good for her to get to know you and your brothers and see your relationship."

His shoulders relaxed and he smiled at her. "She's a great kid."

"She is," Eve agreed. "What happened last night at the hospital?"

His eyes darted to her face. She didn't look angry, so why did he feel instantly defensive? Then he realized— this wasn't about him, not for Eve. It was about Alice. He took a mental step back. The least he could do was try to explain.

"Before you and Alice moved to the ranch, I thought I'd made some progress. I thought I'd finally accepted what happened to my family and I was moving forward. Pretty funny, huh?"

Her gaze didn't waver from his.

He cleared his throat. "Turns out that being with y'all has brought up some feelings I wasn't expecting, some memories I thought I'd put away."

When her eyes softened in pity, he shook his head. "Don't look at me like that. It's just a thing, you know?"

"I do know." She paused. "Tanner, if you need to take some time—"

"I don't. I..." The thought of it made his breath seize in his chest. "I don't. I'm just out of practice, that's all."

"With people? Feelings?"

He wondered if the misery he was feeling was evident on his face. "All of the above."

Eve laughed. "Fair enough. Next time—if there is a

next time—just tell me if you're feeling overwhelmed. I really do get it."

"I know. I'll try."

Eve patted him on the leg and went to join Alice at the altar. He watched as she and Alice had an in-depth conversation about the baby Jesus not being in the manger yet.

For all the teasing she'd done about his bah-humbug attitude, he had to admit that if there was Christmas spirit to be found, it was here, but not just in the church. In the manger scene. The expectation of the baby who would come to bring forgiveness to the world.

And in Eve, who continued to offer grace, even when it was unexpected and undeserved.

Eve separated the block of pine straw she and Alice had picked up from a roadside truck and tucked it around the bushes in her front bed. With Alice feeling better and her own determination not to look at her finances until she had a plan to fix them, she decided some physical labor would take her mind off everything—including the awkward conversation with Tanner last night.

Donning her work gloves, she'd gotten to work on the flower beds in front of the cottage while Alice played on the porch.

The boxwoods were trimmed, the weeds yanked out by their roots. She'd gotten dirty, worked up a sweat and worked off some of her anxiety about what was to come.

She took a few steps back and got the big picture. Yeah, better. Classy. Her Christmas lights and garland were still adorably tacky, and the combination made her smile. "Hey, Ali-Cat, you still good?"

"Can I have a snack?"

"Oh, Alice, I'm so dirty and it's almost lunchtime, so let's wait, please." She held her breath waiting for the whine, but it didn't come. "I'm going to clean out the gutters along the front porch so the rain doesn't mess up our fresh pine straw, and then I'll come in and fix us both some lunch."

"Okay." Eve could hear Alice humming along with the Christmas carols as she played. *Parents make sacrifices. And it's worth it*, she reminded herself. *Even if they don't know how they're going to pay the bills since their T-shirt stock burned up in a fire.*

Still worth it.

Eve dragged the ladder that had been hanging around on the side of the house since she'd borrowed it out of the farm shed and leaned it against the porch roof. She could toss the leaves and stuff onto the blue tarp she'd been using for the weeds and then throw all of it away at the same time.

As she dug her fingers into the cruddy mess and tossed it down on the tarp, she replayed the conversation from last night. Why hadn't Tanner just told her how he was feeling the other night at the hospital?

He definitely wasn't great at making his feelings known. Even though he'd tried to share last night, his words had been so vague. *It's just a thing.* And after all, what really was between them? They'd shared a kiss. A pretty awesome kiss, but so what? It didn't mean he owed her anything.

Maybe he was just being friendly, checking in on her and Alice, and she should've just kept her mouth shut about the whole thing. That seemed the most likely scenario.

One thing she couldn't explain away was how he'd won Alice's trust. That was what made her bring up his hasty departure from the hospital in the first place. So how did she reconcile her concern for Alice with Tanner's... Tanner's what? Fear?

"What are you doing up there?"

Eve froze.

"Seriously, Eve, what are you doing?"

Without loosening her grip or changing her balance, she turned around. Tanner squinted up at her from the front walkway. His arms were crossed, and she wondered if she was about to see his version of "angry man."

"It seems obvious to me that I cleaned out the flower beds and now I'm cleaning out the gutter." She wiggled her fingers. "Got the dirt on my gloves to prove it."

"If it needed to be done, why didn't you ask me?"

Eve made her way—carefully—down the ladder and walked over to Tanner, hands still in her work gloves now fisted on her hips. "Why would I do that when I'm perfectly capable of making minor repairs? In fact, it's in my rental agreement that I'll do them."

"I didn't say you weren't capable," he started.

She glared at him. "Who do you think fixes the toilet for me when it breaks? Or unclogs a sink? If there's a big scary bug, guess who kills it?"

With a glance over at Alice, who was watching intently from the porch, he lowered his voice in the way she was starting to realize revealed his feelings more than if he'd raised it in a shout. And that, frankly, melted her annoyance with him just a little. "I hear you. You are capable. You're downright amazing. I mean it. All I'm saying is, you don't have to do this alone now that you have me in your life."

Eve went still. She locked her gaze on his. "*Do* I have you in my life?"

As she stood toe-to-toe with him, Tanner blanched. And then, in his very measured tone, said, "It's not fair of me to say that. I know what my gut's telling me, but you deserve better than that. You deserve a real answer. I'm just not sure I have one. I'm sorry."

As she stood there with her mouth hanging open, he turned and walked away.

She glanced at her watch and smothered a shout. "Alice, we've got to get a move on. It's almost time to go. You're going to Gramma and Grampa's house for the afternoon, and I have to go get ready for the party on Saturday!"

The whole team of people they'd assembled was supposed to meet at the big fellowship hall in town this afternoon to make decorations for the party on Saturday. They wouldn't be able to recreate her whole vision, but between the contacts she'd made and Wynn Grant's, they'd managed to have almost everything donated to throw a fabulous party.

Now all they had to do was pull it off. She had to concentrate on that, even with her insides churning from this latest conversation with Tanner, if you could call it that.

As she took the fastest shower in history and wrestled Alice into clothes, Tanner's words—*you don't have to do this alone now that you have me in your life*—were on repeat in her mind.

Along with her own lingering question: What was between them, anyway? Were they just friends? Were they more?

She honestly had no idea.

Chapter Fourteen

Tanner opened the door of the fellowship hall at the church in town and was hit by a wall of Christmas cheer that knocked him back three steps. Chatter, Christmas carols, pealing laughter. And if this is what the preparations looked like, the party should be really…fun. He'd come a long way, but he wasn't sure he was prepared for this level of holiday spirit.

Whether he was or wasn't, though, Triple Creek Ranch had volunteered to host this party. It might not have turned out the way they'd expected, but he wasn't going to renege on a commitment, especially one they'd made to help give kids in foster care a special memory.

"Merry Christmas, Tanner!" Mrs. Berryhill, his high school English teacher, called across the room. She and a few of the other ladies had been busy making faux peppermint-candy decorations. She held one over her head and wiggled it.

"Thanks, Mrs. B. Same to you." As he walked deeper into the room, Tanner took off his hat and ran his hand through his hair. Finally, he spotted Eve sitting on the edge of the stage with Wynn, their heads—one dark, one blond—together over a clipboard.

A group of women had sorted the T-shirts Eve had made for the kids—now being kept safely under her kitchen table—into family groups and rolled and tied them with ribbons and gift tags. It had been Eve's brilliant idea to color code the shirts to keep kids moving through the different stations.

"Tanner! Good to see you! Merry Christmas! So nice of the ranch to sponsor this event for the kids." Pastor Jake was stuffing food baskets with napkins and his wife, Ellen, was following him with bags of chips.

"Our pleasure. I'm just sorry we couldn't have it at the ranch, but we appreciate you opening the doors of the church to get things ready."

Wynn pointed at something across the room, and as Eve looked up, her gaze caught on his. There was a flash of something in her eyes, but he had no clue what it was. Maybe it was interest. Could just as easily have been irritation. He had no idea.

He kept hearing the words he'd said earlier on repeat and seeing her face as he turned away. She hadn't looked shattered. No, she'd looked…resigned. Like maybe she'd expected that from him. He'd thought about skipping the party preparation completely, but he couldn't do that to Eve. She'd worked so hard, and she deserved his full support.

But inside, he was quaking. Because while she hadn't known what he was thinking when she'd asked him if she had him in her life, he did. He'd been stunned into silence—not because it scared him, but because his answer, his gut response, was an unequivocal *yes*.

He blinked, the room coming back into focus. The whole place smelled like the sugar cookies a group of ladies were baking for the kids to decorate. His stomach growled as he edged closer to Eve.

"Tanner, we were so sorry to hear about your barn. I hope things are going to be okay for you." Mary Pat Haney put her hand on his arm. Garrett had set them up on a blind date a few years back. It had been a disaster, but Mary Pat was as sweet as they came, and she'd never tried to hold it against him.

"It's just a setback, that's all. Thanks for asking, though, Mary Pat."

After being stopped two more times, Tanner finally reached the stage and Eve. "Hey."

"Hey, yourself. Thanks for stopping by." She looked up at him, her eyes shining, cheeks pink with excitement.

In contrast, still reeling from their earlier meeting, he felt slow, his tongue thick in his mouth. "Is there anything I can do?"

She raised an eyebrow with a smirk. "I'm just impressed that you haven't run screaming from the building yet, what with all this Christmas spirit."

"You're hilarious," he said drily. So, apparently they were going to pretend the conversation earlier today hadn't happened, which was fine by him. "What can I do to help?"

She glanced at her watch. "We're about to wrap up here, and my in-laws will be dropping Alice off. Lacey's been overseeing the cookie baking and coordinating the packaging of the cookie decorating kits, so she's probably exhausted. How do you feel about picking up a few pizzas and meeting us back at the house?"

"You want me to leave?" He narrowed his eyes. "Is this a trick?"

Eve laughed, but she shook her head. "Nope. I know you'd rather do just about anything rather than be in this room full of cheerfully nosy church people. No offense, Wynn."

Wynn glanced up. "None taken."

Eve had surprised him, throwing him off-kilter— again. And if there'd ever been a question whether she got him, there wasn't a question now. He managed a half smile. "Any requests?"

"Cheese for me and Alice."

"Pepperoni for me and—" he shuddered "—ham and pineapple for Devin and Lacey. Wynn?"

"Oh, no. I promised Latham I'd be home for supper tonight, but thanks."

One of the women who was working on the decorations called out to Eve, who slid off the stage with her clipboard in hand. "Meet you at home?"

"I'll see you there." To Wynn, Tanner said, "We couldn't have made any of this happen without you. Thanks for pitching in."

"It's a good cause and good for the town. But it's your girl there who made it happen. She's got great ideas and she's got the know-how to pull them off, too. I'm thinking of hiring her to coordinate Spring Fling this year. Or, more likely, begging her to coordinate Spring Fling this year."

"That would be great."

"She's pretty special. But how do *you* feel about her?"

Tanner studied Wynn's suddenly guileless expression. He'd known her a long time. He was older, so he'd been better friends with her older brothers, but it was a small town. If you had a life, everybody was all up in your business. Some things never changed.

"She—" He hesitated. How did he tell Wynn how he felt when he didn't even understand it himself? "—throws me off balance."

Wynn laughed. "Balance is overrated, my friend. Latham Grant has been throwing me off-kilter since we teamed up to annoy my brother in middle school. And as it turned out, he's everything I never knew I needed."

Tanner shifted his weight, uneasy with the personal turn of this conversation. "I'm not sure that's a fair comparison."

Wynn's eyes met his with a challenge. "Just don't give up without trying, okay? You deserve it. So does she."

"Thanks, Wynn. I'll see you at the party."

As he walked over to the Hilltop Café to pick up the pizza, he thought about all the good Eve and Alice brought to his life. He hadn't looked for it. Definitely hadn't expected it, but Eve brought joy—anticipation—that he'd thought he'd never have again. Maybe it was time to tell her that.

Sitting on the floor, her back against the sofa, Eve leaned forward to grab her third piece of pizza from the box on the coffee table. She was starving after smelling cookies baking all afternoon. It had been a difficult exercise not to raid the kitchen after everyone left.

Lacey held her feet up for Devin to put a pillow underneath them. "I have to say, after the barn burned down, I wasn't sure we were going to be able to pull everything together to have the party."

"Well, *we* didn't pull it together," Devin said.

"Exactly what I was about to say. All those people showing up to help today and being so excited about the party restores my faith in humanity."

"I was terrified no one was going to show up." Eve bit a chunk off the crust. "Until they actually did, I was convinced we were going to have a bare park with some balloons and a couple of bouncy houses. Maybe the kids wouldn't have minded much, but it definitely wasn't what I envisioned."

The twins were bathed and in bed, and Eve could hear one of them talking over the monitor. Alice was asleep by the fire with her head on Sadie's back, a half-eaten piece of pizza in her hand. She'd apparently spent the entire visit with her grandparents chasing the puppies around the yard. Once her belly was full, she'd passed out.

Devin flopped onto the sofa. "The people in this town love a good project."

"Good thing they do." Tanner took a swig of a soda. "Or we'd be up a creek."

Tanner had been very quiet. She studied his face, wondering. Was this more than his normal Tanner quiet, or maybe she should just stop overthinking it?

"Wynn is scary organized." Eve tossed the last bite of her crust onto the empty box and licked her fingers.

"Funny. She said the same thing about you," Tanner said.

"Oh, that's so nice." Eve beamed.

"Careful, Eve. That's how you get roped into volunteering to be on one of Wynn's famous work teams." Lacey's voice was serious. "Trust me on this."

Tanner grinned. "Oh, I think it's already too late for Eve. Mayor Grant has got your number."

Eve laughed. "Well, on that note, I'm heading home. I need to get the peanut into bed. Tomorrow is going to come early."

"I'll run y'all home in the ATV," Tanner said.

"Devin said he'd drive us, but thank you." Not that she was avoiding being alone with Tanner. She wasn't, exactly. Eve pushed to her feet. "I'm so sore from pulling weeds in the flower bed this morning, I can barely lift my arms."

She turned around to find Devin already sound asleep on the couch, his hat pulled down over his eyes. Lacey laughed. "He's gonna wake up at ten o'clock tonight and think it's time to get up for the day."

"Looks like you're stuck with me," Tanner said. "Grab a blanket off the back of the couch, and I'll get Alice. It's gonna be a chilly ride."

Eve nodded, and Tanner reached down for Alice, effortlessly lifting her and carrying her toward the door. Her heart squeezed as Alice's skinny little arms circled Tanner's neck. Whatever Eve's feelings for Tanner were, and those were still to be determined, Alice had fallen hard for the handsome rancher.

"See you tomorrow, Eve." Lacey kicked back farther in the recliner and closed her eyes.

Feeling nostalgic, Eve picked up one of the throw blankets from the back of the sofa. She remembered the feeling of being pregnant and so exhausted you could barely move. But she also remembered how her heart had leaped the first time she'd felt Alice move.

She'd loved every second of it.

Eve followed Tanner outside and climbed into the ATV, holding her arms out. He placed Alice in her lap, wrapping the blanket around both of them.

He slid in beside her. "No heat. Sorry."

"No walls, either. It's cold now that the sun went down." She shivered.

Turning the key, he cranked the engine and pulled slowly out into the lane, Sadie trotting along beside them. "Yeah, but those stars are worth it."

They were. With no city lights to dim them, the stars weren't simply tiny twinkling lights in the sky—they were mysterious and vast, stretching for what seemed like infinity. "It's so beautiful."

When they reached the cottage, Tanner came around to pick Alice up again and followed Eve up the steps. "I'll put her in bed."

Eve followed him down the hall to Alice's tiny bedroom, watching as Tanner laid her gently on the bed, his movements as careful as if he were dealing with dynamite or delicate china.

He retreated, and Eve slid Alice out of her dirty clothes and into some pj's. Grumbling, Alice burrowed into her covers as Sadie jumped up beside her and made her own nest.

When she returned to the living room, Tanner had turned on the lights on the tree and had his back to the fireplace, where a fire was burning merrily. She walked over to stand beside him, facing the fire, and wished she knew what was going on in his mind. "Still no Christmas spirit?"

"Maybe a little," he admitted. He looked down at her, wry amusement in his dark brown eyes.

She laughed softly. "Still holding out. Well, you still have a few more days to find it."

"Will Alice go to the party on Saturday?"

"Good question. I don't know. I'll talk to her about it in the morning, but I think there's a good chance she'll want to go to her grandparents' instead. She just isn't ready for a big crowd with a lot of noise."

"The library's right next to the park. Maybe she could come for a little while and leave if it gets over-whelming for her. Or she could watch from the library and join in if she feels like it."

"That's such a good idea. She's a quirky kid, especially after all she's been through, but you seem to have a knack for figuring out what she needs. I'm grateful."

"Eve…" His eyes were on hers and her breath hitched as she realized he was maybe, finally, going to kiss her.

He slid one hand into her hair and pulled her toward him. As she moved closer to him, she lifted her chin, letting their lips meet, her eyes drifting closed.

When he pulled away, he didn't go far. "You have me in your life, Eve, if you want me. I'm not sure what it means, but I'm here."

She let her head fall against his chest and stood there, his arms surrounding her. She felt so at peace and so… safe, here, with the crackle of the fireplace and the glow of the lights from the tree surrounding them.

Eve didn't want to move, to break the moment with him, but soon he eased back. "I'm not an easy person,

Eve. I'm moody and private and, according to reputable sources, *very* opinionated."

"I'm not afraid." She touched his face with her hand, rubbing her thumb across that crease in his cheek that deepened when he was amused. "You have me in your life, too. If you want me."

"If I—" He laughed softly as he wrapped his arms around her, lifting her off the ground to hold her in a tight embrace. "I haven't been able to think about anything else all day."

Somewhere in the back of her mind, she wondered if he'd thought through all the complicated aspects of her life, and his, but she didn't say anything. Not now. Tonight she was content just to be.

He wasn't making any promises.

She didn't know if she wanted them. But if he was willing to take a chance on the two of them, she was in.

Because if she'd learned anything from loving Brent, from loving Alice and Maribeth and Henry, too…it was that love was worth it.

Even when it hurt.

Chapter Fifteen

Eve stood off to the side watching, like a general overseeing a battle, as her plan unfolded. The kids were rotating from ornament painting to cookie decorating to lunch to the bouncy houses with their group leaders. Even the parents were having fun as they followed their kids around, taking pictures and chatting.

"It's going well," Wynn Grant said, standing next to her.

There was the occasional screamer, of course. These were children, after all. She'd planned for that, too, assigning one of the volunteers to swoop in to deliver a candy cane and a sticker in case of emergency. There had been a lot of emergencies.

She grinned, glancing at Wynn. "So far, so good."

Tanner was picking up trash as each group left their station to move to the next. She studied his easy smile as one of the parents spoke to him. You'd never know he'd rather be anywhere but here.

Wynn leaned in. "He's a heartbreaker."

"I'll say." Wynn's sister, Jules, stood nearby, a baby on her hip. "Can't tell you how many women over the years have had their cap set for that handsome cowboy."

"There're gonna be even more hearts broken now that he's off the market," Wynn said, a wry tone to her voice.

"Off the market?" Eve looked at Wynn in surprise. "What makes you say that?"

"Just intuition. But I'm curious about you. How do you feel about him?"

A sweaty toddler did a face-plant coming out of a bouncy house and let out a high-pitched wail.

"Oh no. That's one of mine. Here, Wynn, take her." Jules handed the baby to Wynn and jogged toward the crying child.

Wynn didn't flinch, just hitched the baby up on her hip. "So?"

Eve squinted her eyes and scrunched her nose. "Let's just say he's got me all tied up in knots."

Wynn laughed. "Sounds like love to me."

"Eve!" Pastor Jake hustled over. "We ran out of chips. I'm not sure how that happened. I thought we had one in each lunch basket."

"There are some extras under the check-in table in the blue plastic tub, just in case."

"Okay, thanks, whew." Pastor Jake grinned. "Crisis averted."

As he walked away, Wynn turned to Eve, swaying slightly with the baby in her arms. "On another subject, I know you've just started your graphic design business, but I'd be interested in talking to you about coordinating the Spring Fling. It wouldn't pay much, but enough maybe to supplement your income until you get on your feet. You really are good at this."

Pleased and surprised, Eve didn't hesitate. "I'd love to. I don't even have to think about it. Event planning is my passion, but I knew Alice needed time with me, so I started the T-shirt business as a way to work from home."

"If you can do what you did today on a shoestring budget and in such a short time—from home—I think you'll have all the business you can handle." As someone called her, the mayor lifted her hand and waved. "Duty calls. I'll see you later. Here."

She passed the baby to Eve and walked away. Eve looked down at the little one all decked out in a red-and-green Christmas dress and a bow that had to be twice the size of her head. Wide blue eyes blinked back at her. "Hi there, munchkin. Guess what? I think I got a job."

"Mama!" A little voice called Eve's name just as that little body hit her legs.

Her father-in-law, Henry, breathing fast, arrived right behind Alice. "She's been watching how much fun the kids are having. She wanted to come down and play a little bit, if that's okay with you."

"Of course it's okay." Eve smiled down at Alice, who'd agreed to wear her own Christmas outfit—a green sweatshirt made by Eve and ruffled red leggings—instead of her typical princess dress.

"Whose baby is that?" Before Eve could answer, Alice said, "There's Mr. Tanner! Can I go see him?"

"Sure." Eve laughed and turned to her mother-in-law as she caught up to Henry. "She's certainly found her voice."

Maribeth put her arm around Eve as Alice reached Tanner, who lifted her up into his arms and pretended to drop her. "She's doing so well. You were right—the farm life suits her. She's thriving."

"Yes, she is, but it's not just farm life. Part of the reason she's doing so well is that she has both of you in her life." The baby in Eve's arms rubbed her eyes, and Eve patted her tiny back, bouncing up and down.

Maribeth glanced at Henry and back to Eve. "We need to apologize. You have your own life, you and Alice, and we want to support you, not try to make decisions for you."

"I appreciate that." Eve turned toward her mother-in-law, reaching for her hand. "But you and Henry have nothing to apologize for. You've supported me every step of the way."

Maribeth looked toward the playground, her eyes filling. "We want you to be happy, Eve. Whatever that means for you."

Eve followed Maribeth's eyes to where Tanner had swung Alice over his head. Her squeals of laughter were clear, even over all of the hubbub surrounding them. "Thank you. You have no idea how much I needed to hear you say that."

"We're gonna head home if you've got things covered here." Henry put his arm around his wife then pulled a small figure out of his pocket and handed it to Eve. "Alice really wanted to bring the baby Jesus from our nativity home with her, and we told her she could have it."

"Are you sure?" When he nodded, she hugged them

both. "I love you. We'll see you bright and early Christmas morning."

"Bye, sweetie." Maribeth smiled through her tears and quickly walked away with Henry at her side.

The baby girl's eyes were bobbing closed, so Eve shifted her to her shoulder as she made her way to the table at the entrance. Families were beginning to trickle out, and Eve wanted to stand by the table at the exit where Lacey had been printing out Santa photos as fast as the photographer was taking them.

Claire, one of the foster moms, stood nearby as her eight kids found their pictures. "This was wonderful. Even my teenagers had a blast."

"Hearing that makes our day. Thank you!"

Jules rushed up, gripping one small child by the hand and carrying the toddler on her hip. Another child trailed behind her. "Oh good, you've got the baby. I was starting to think I'd lost her."

Eve laughed. "Can we help you get to the car?"

"My husband is around here somewhere." Jules scanned the park. "There he is. Cam, over here!"

Her husband strolled up with more kids—two girls who looked like they were in early elementary school. "Is that my baby?"

With a grin, Eve said, "Maybe? I'm not sure."

Jules shook her head. "It really is hard to keep up. Cameron, this is Eve. She and her daughter are renting the cottage where Garrett used to live. Eve, Cameron."

"Nice to meet you." Eve handed the sleeping baby over to her dad. And around thirty minutes later, as the last family picked up their photos and wound their way to the parking lot, she breathed a huge sigh of relief.

The cleanup crew had already started breaking things down. Pastor Jake was hauling big tubs out of the church van and into the park, where they were quickly filled with the decorations.

"This was great. I'm exhausted." Lacey stacked up a few straggling photos that hadn't been picked up. "I think I'm gonna head home. Devin snagged some box lunches and stashed them in the car, if you and Alice want to stop by on your way home."

"We'll do that. Thank you so much for your help."

Devin pushed the double stroller ahead of him, but still managed to put his arm around Lacey as they headed to the truck. The strap of the diaper bag started to slide off his shoulder, and Lacey nudged it back into place. Eve sighed. They were so cute.

She picked up the photos and stuck them to her clipboard as a couple of men from the church tipped the table over and broke it down to haul back to the church. "Thanks so much, guys."

Within about twenty minutes, all that remained in the park were the deflated bouncy houses, and those would be picked up by the various vendors by late afternoon.

Tanner walked over to her as the last table was being carried out of the park and into the church van. "I can't believe we actually pulled it off."

"We couldn't have done it without all the volunteers from the church, but it turned out great. Thanks for being such a good sport. I know hordes of children—and adults—in various stages of euphoria and meltdown are not exactly your thing."

Tanner bumped her with his shoulder. "It wasn't even too bad, especially once the peanut arrived. She's on the playground. Want me to take her home while you finish up here?"

"Sure. It shouldn't be long, and I'll be finishing up soon."

She was doing the final run-through of her post-party checklist when she heard a little voice call out, "Bye, Mama!"

Alice had Tanner's cowboy hat on as she rode his shoulders to the parking lot, her hands in the air with no fear that Tanner would let her go.

Eve had fallen for Tanner almost as fast as Alice had. Was it any wonder? Despite all he'd lost, his heart was so big and so generous.

One big question mark remained in her mind. Was he ready to move on? Was she?

She packed up her stuff and waved goodbye to the few remaining volunteers. And when she got in her van, she sat in silence for a minute.

She'd taken some huge risks in her life. Starting her own business and moving to Alabama topped the list. But falling in love with Tanner?

That might be the biggest risk of all.

Tanner sat on the front porch at the farmhouse with his legs stretched out in front of him, the bottle-feeding piglet dribbling milk all over his legs. The weather had warmed up nicely, a pleasant sixty-eight degrees. It was supposed to get even warmer at the beginning of the week. It wasn't very Christmassy weather, but the cows liked it, and he'd take it.

Alice was digging with a stick in the driveway, twin babies toddling around her, with Devin sitting on the bottom step keeping watch. "Eli, no-no. Rocks don't go in your mouth."

Eli opened his mouth, and a shower of pebbles fell to the ground.

Devin got up and wiped Eli's mouth with his shirt-tail. "I thought newborns were hard. Toddlers are constantly doing things that could land you in the ER."

"They're cute, though." Abby had stuck Charlotte into one of those baby seats that rocked and bounced and was handing her animal crackers one at a time. Garrett was half-asleep sitting in one of the porch chairs beside her.

Tanner leaned his head back against the rail. This had been one wild month, but he was here with his brothers and their families and, while he would always regret that his parents and his wife and son weren't here, he could also be…grateful.

He *was* grateful. He'd watched Eve at the party today, how effortlessly she connected with people and managed the minor crises that popped up. He'd never expected to have someone like her in his life. Getting to know her, being in her life… For the first time in a long time, he was considering what the future could look like as a family of three.

Alice and Eve were good for him. They were good together.

Eve pulled up in her van, parked beside the house and walked over to join them on the porch. She threw her arms up in the air. "Whew! We did it!"

Garrett laughed. "I still can't believe the party came together like that."

"Me, either." Lacey was in the swing, one leg dangling over the edge to keep it moving. "You did a fantastic job organizing everything, Eve."

Charlotte squealed, and Abby handed her another cracker. "I think people like doing things like this. I see it all the time during disasters. What should be the worst of times brings out the best in people."

"Well, it was amazing." Eve flopped on the floor next to Tanner, smiling up at him as he put his arm around her. "Hi."

"Hi." He grinned as, out of the corner of his eye, he caught his brothers sharing a wide-eyed look between them.

"I even got a job out of it, I think. Wynn asked if I would sign on to coordinate the town's Spring Fling." Her tone was buoyant.

"That's fantastic. I bet that's a weight off your shoulders." Garrett's eyes were on Tanner's hand, where his fingers rubbed Eve's shoulder.

"It is. But right now, I'm just so happy this party is over and it was a success."

"It was a huge success," Lacey said. "The kids were so cute. Even the teenagers had fun."

"I've never been so tired in my life," Devin said.

"Really?" Eve laughed. "Not me. I love kids."

Tanner's fingers went still. Did Eve want more children? He'd seen her at the park with Jules's baby, and she'd seemed so at ease. A complete natural.

With his thoughts spinning, he almost missed Garrett saying, "If I ever start talking about having more kids, remind me that I'm perfectly fine with Charlotte being an only child."

Abby swung her head around toward Garrett, both

eyebrows raised. "Well, then, I guess this is a bad time for me to tell you we're expecting?"

The blood drained from Garrett's face.

Devin started laughing. "You should see your expression."

"I don't know what you're laughing at. You're well on your way to a dozen kids already." Garrett grabbed his wife's hands and pulled her into his lap, his expression goofy with love. "We're having a baby?"

She nodded, and Garrett whooped. "We're having a baby!"

"When are you due?" Lacey asked.

"The same week you are."

"Our babies are going to be best friends." Lacey started crying, which made Abby cry.

Tanner was happy. Of course he was. *For them.* But being happy for them wasn't the same as being ready, prepared, to have his heart walking around outside his body again. He'd taken a huge risk opening himself up to care about Eve and Alice.

He was still feeling his way there. Loving more. Risking more. If something happened, he wouldn't survive it.

"We have to celebrate! I'm going to throw you two the best baby shower ever." Eve was laughing, clearly delighted with the whole thing. "It will be so amazing for Charlotte to have a brother or sister."

"It will." Abby leaned in to Garrett as he kissed her on the head. "I was an only child, and I always wanted a sibling."

"Me, too." Eve's face melted into a nostalgic smile.

"If things had been different, I'd have loved for Alice to have a sibling. Maybe one day."

Tanner tensed at her words, his sense of panic building to a tight knot in his chest.

"I'm not gonna lie, guys, pregnancy is not always a walk in the park," Lacey chimed in. "But when you feel that baby move, you'll be in love, and it'll all be worth it."

"You haven't slept in the nine months Charlotte's been here. What's another year or two with no sleep?" Devin said.

Tanner had to get out of here. He handed Eve the pig and pushed to his feet, hoping they'd just see his departure as shying away from all the baby talk. He forced a smile. "Congratulations, guys. Proud to have another Cole joining the crew."

Without saying another word, he jogged down the steps and started down the lane, the voices on the porch fading as he got farther away, the voices in his head just growing louder.

How could you let yourself get in this position?

So what if you love her?

And perhaps the most devastating of all:

You couldn't protect the family you had.

What makes you think you deserve another one?

Chapter Sixteen

Eve stared after Tanner as he strode down the gravel road leading to the back of the property. Behind her, the rest of the family had gone quiet. She turned toward them. "What just happened?"

"No clue." Garrett had his arm wrapped around Abby, one hand on her still-flat stomach. "Maybe the pregnancy talk? I don't know—I thought he was getting better with stuff like this."

"I'll go talk to him if someone will watch the kids." Devin stood.

"No, I'll go, if you don't mind." Eve looked from one to the others of Tanner's family and started down the steps. "Any idea where he's gone?"

Devin held his hands out, and she handed him the pig as she reached the bottom of the stairs. "My best guess is the spring. If you take the trail to the pond and go around it, there's a path through the woods to where the head of the spring is. Our mom used to go there sometimes."

"Thanks." Eve tapped Alice on the shoulder. "Stick close to the house, okay? And listen to the grown-ups. I'll be back soon."

"Can I come?" Alice had somehow found Sadie's nasty tennis ball and was bouncing it to the patient dog.

"Not this time. I'll be back soon." She dropped a kiss on her baby's head and started down the gravel drive.

Following Devin's instructions, she rounded the corner by the pasture and took the trail around the pond. As she walked, she replayed the conversation in her mind. He *had* tensed when they started talking about babies and pregnancy.

But why?

Her footsteps slowed as she reached the far side of the pond until, finally, she spotted a faint trail leading into the woods.

She took a few careful steps through the trees and saw him sitting in a faded and peeling wooden Adirondack chair, gazing at a stream that bubbled and whispered across a sandy floor.

He spoke without greeting her. "This was my mom's favorite spot to escape. I wish I could talk to her right now. Sometimes, when I come around that corner, I imagine she'll be sitting in this chair with an open book in her lap. I miss her. I miss them."

Eve's annoyance eased. She put her hand on his shoulder and he looked up. "How do you do it, Eve?"

"Do what?"

"Love so fiercely, without fear suffocating you." He paused, his eyes returning to the crystal clear water where it bubbled up out of the ground. "Sometimes I feel like the whole world is moving forward at this superfast pace, and I'm standing still while it goes on without me."

"Because your brothers are married and having babies?"

"Maybe." He looked down. "I want to be happy for them. I *am* happy for them, but I'm also scared for them."

Her eyebrows drawing together, she opened her mouth to ask why he was afraid, but then he spoke again, his words slow and measured, almost hesitant. "Did you really mean it when you said you wanted more kids someday?"

"Is my off-the-cuff comment about that what's really bothering you?"

"Maybe. Yes? Do you?"

She needed to handle this carefully. Tanner's body was coiled, like a spring about to explode into motion, every muscle tight and tense. "If it works out for me, I want more someday, yes. I love being a mom. Talk to me, Tanner. Tell me what you're thinking."

He didn't move. His voice, when it came, was low but shaking with the effort to keep it steady. "I care about you and Alice, more than I ever thought I could or would. But I don't want any more children. I just… can't imagine being okay with all those pieces of my heart running around. It might sound stupid, but I—I don't know if I can handle loving more."

He looked and sounded miserable.

"I understand where you're coming from. There was a time when I thought I'd never fall in love again because what came later was just too painful." She froze.

She hadn't meant to say that, but he either didn't hear her or chose to ignore her.

She knelt in front of him, putting her hands on his knees. "Listen to me. What you're feeling isn't weird. It's not even conscious thought. Your brain is just trying to protect you."

Tanner looked skeptical. His eyes were dark with pain, but he kept them trained on hers, like a lifeline.

Eve searched her memory for what she'd learned about PTSD during her counseling sessions after Brent died. "It's a fight-or-flight response, a reflex. Tanner, you experienced a horrible tragedy. People call what happens a broken heart, and maybe it is, but there are also pathways in the brain that are changed forever. When you feel protective of something, your brain says, *wait a minute, remember what happened last time? Run.*"

He looked down with a chuckle, but it was a forced, mirthless sound.

"The important thing to remember is that pathways can be rerouted. *You* are not broken." She turned her hands up on his knees, willing him to hear her, willing him to reach out and grab her hands.

"I'm not sure that's true." He snapped his head up, his gaze suddenly intense on hers. "I couldn't protect them, and I don't know what to do with that."

"That's not how the universe works, Tanner. Love or no love, sometimes things just happen. What matters is that your wife and your baby knew they were loved. There's no doubt in my mind about that."

He pushed to his feet and paced away from her, wiping his face with his hands before turning around. "We have to stop this—whatever *this* is between us—before it's too late. I don't want you to get hurt." Her bottom lip trembled, and his eyes softened. He reached for her, and she took a step back, out of his reach. "Eve—"

"Wow, you have some really spectacular timing." She took a ragged breath and looked down with a smile, gathering her thoughts before she met his eyes again. "A week ago, I might've agreed with you that we should stop this…whatever it is…before anyone gets hurt. Now?"

He was shaking his head slowly, as if he didn't want to hear her words, but tears brimmed in his eyes again.

What matters is they knew they were loved. As she'd said the words, she'd known they were true. As people, humans, they could only do so much, only influence so much. The rest was out of their control.

But this? This she could control. He would know he was loved.

She took a deep breath. "I love you, Tanner Cole. And you can turn away from that if you like, but do it because you don't feel the same way, not because you're too afraid to love again. You *deserve* to be happy. You deserve to know love."

He blanched. "I don't know what you want me to say."

Forcing a shaky smile, Eve held her palms up, hands wide. "I don't want you to say anything."

What she wanted was for him to hold her, to wrap her in his familiar, steady embrace. She wanted him to tell her not to worry, to say that everything would be okay.

And she wanted, more than anything, for her heart—for Alice's heart—to be safe with him.

But he couldn't ensure that, not now. So she turned and walked away, not because she was angry, but because there was nothing more she could do.

Two hours later, after the evening chores were finished, Tanner walked slowly back to the farmhouse. Garrett's SUV was gone, and the front porch was empty. Through the bare winter trees, he could see the lights on at the cottage, but for the first time, they didn't feel welcoming to him.

He opened the door and stepped inside.

Devin looked up from a bent-over position where he was tossing toys into a basket with Eli, wearing a zip-up sleeper, on the floor nearby. "You back?"

Tanner thought for a minute. "Cows are fed. Horses, too. Goats. Pigs. So…yeah."

His brother picked Eli up from the floor and followed him into the kitchen, watching as Tanner washed his hands and dried them. "You okay?"

"Not so much."

"Want to talk about it?"

"No."

"Good. Lacey was exhausted and went to bed early, and I need to get Phoebe ready for bed." Devin handed Tanner the baby and disappeared down the hall.

Tanner sighed.

He looked down at Eli, who stared at him solemnly, his thumb in his mouth. Tanner patted the little back, grabbed an apple off the table and walked back through the living room and outside. In his experience, little people preferred the outdoors to being inside, no matter how many toys there were to play with.

With Eli on his arm, he walked across the driveway to the pasture where Toby and Reggie were grazing. "See that big brown horse, Eli? That one's Toby. He's a worker. Never gets tired. He does get annoyed with the calves sometimes, though. The other horse, that's Reggie, but you know him. He's your dad's horse. Best cow horse I've ever seen. Don't tell your dad I said this, but Reggie is the real reason your dad won all those titles."

With a small smile, he glanced down at Eli, who blinked at him with big brown eyes. "Don't tell him this, either, but I've never seen anyone as natural with horses as your dad is. He's pretty special."

With the rodeo genes Eli and Phoebe had gotten from their parents, it seemed likely that the twins would be on horseback before long. It made him want to wrap them in cotton and duct tape and follow them around with a pillow.

Even as he thought it, he realized how ridiculous it sounded, but still, his arms closed tightly around the baby. His wife and son had flown safely on an airplane across the country to visit her grandmother, and then they'd been killed in a car accident five miles from home.

It was senseless.

Toby ambled over to the fence, and Tanner held the small apple out for him. When Toby took the apple with his gigantic teeth, Eli's thumb came unglued from his mouth, his rapt attention on the horse. "Toby likes apples and carrots, just like you, buddy."

The sound of little footsteps pounding his way caught his ear. He glanced around in time to see Alice running down the road, her princess dress—pink this time—floating along behind her.

"Mr. Tanner, Mr. Tanner!"

"Alice?" He looked behind her but saw no sign of Eve. "Does your mom know you're here?"

She shook her head, her blond curls bouncing. "I made you a picture."

"You did?" He crouched down so that he was almost eye level with her as she handed it to him. "Is this a rainbow? It's beautiful."

"Rainbows make me happy when I'm sad." Her expression was earnest.

"You think I'm sad?"

She nodded her head vehemently. "Mama said."

Eli kicked his feet, not sure he liked their current position. Tanner stood and settled Eli back on his arm. "Thank you very much for this picture. I am a little sad, but your drawing makes me feel better. It's really special."

He looked up as he heard Eve calling for Alice. "Your mom is looking for you. You better run home now before you get too cold."

Alice flashed a grin and ran back toward the cottage, giving a little skip once in a while. He looked down at the picture in his hand. Underneath the rainbow, she'd drawn three figures—a very small one, a medium-size one and a very tall one in an unmistakable cowboy hat.

Tanner cleared his throat. How in the world did he handle that?

He followed along behind her, not so close that she would know, until he turned the corner toward the cottage and his footsteps slowed. Eve was standing on the porch, hands on her hips, as Alice ran toward her. She listened for a minute, and then she lifted her head, her eyes seeking his out.

With a pitiful excuse for a smile, he lifted a hand. She gave a half-hearted wave in return.

It was almost more than he could do to turn away from them and walk back to the farmhouse, but he couldn't lead her on. He wanted to believe what she said today. Wanted so badly to believe that he could change the way he thought about love. Risk. Heartbreak.

Eli laid his head on Tanner's shoulder, his little body growing heavy on Tanner's arm. He looked down at the picture that Alice had drawn, though it had grown too dark to see the details. These children were so precious. They enriched his life in ways he couldn't even describe. Would he really wish he hadn't known them even if the worst happened?

Of course he wouldn't. As he turned back toward home, his footsteps were heavy with sadness. He'd been frozen in self-protection mode for so long and the thaw had happened so slowly that he'd barely noticed until it was too late.

So now he faced a choice. He could continue on the way he had been, shore up the walls, shut people out of his life. Or he could take a chance. And…spend his life living on the edge of terror.

He closed his eyes and swayed for a moment, with the baby in his arms, and prayed. *Please, Lord. Please help me be strong enough to make the right decision.*

Because he was pretty sure that either way, it was going to hurt.

* * *

"Alice Catherine, time for bed." Eve stood in the door to the tiny second bedroom and waited, her knee jiggling. "Now."

Alice came down the hall, her feet dragging, face scowling. "I don't want to go to bed."

"Hop in. It's cold in here. I'll cover you up and say your prayers with you." As Alice begrudgingly got into the single bed, Eve pulled the heavy covers over her. "It's been such a busy day. Did you have a fun time with Gramma and Grampa this morning?"

"Mmm-hmm." Alice reached under her pillow and pulled out the baby Jesus figurine, cradling it in her pudgy little hand. "Mama, can I get a daddy for Christmas?"

Eve sat back on her heels, tears springing to her eyes. "Oh, Ali-Cat, that's not really how it works. Baby Jesus didn't come to grant wishes. He came so that everyone who knows Him could be close to God, no matter what."

Alice narrowed her eyes. "Like even when that baby pulled my hair today?"

Eve smothered a laugh and managed to keep her smile under wraps. "Yep. No matter what you've done or where you've been, or whose hair you've pulled, you're always welcome in God's family."

Alice tapped her chin, thinking. "I like God's family. And I like my family. I like you and Gramma and Grampa and Sadie and Mr. Tanner. And I like the babies, even when they pull my…"

Her voice trailed off and she yawned, her eyes closing.

"Night, baby girl. I love you."

"Love you, Mama," Alice mumbled.

With her nightly cup of tea, Eve sat down on the yellow couch, thinking about how her life with Brent had started. He'd romanced her, taken her dancing on the beach. They'd laughed. Oh, how they'd laughed. He'd been handsome and chivalrous, and she'd loved him madly.

She had regrets, a whole cartload of them, but loving Brent wasn't one of them. There was still pain, yes. But looking into Alice's eyes and seeing her daddy there... well, it was worth it.

The very last thing she'd expected when she'd moved to Alabama was falling hard for a cowboy whose grumpy exterior hid a heart that was bigger than even he knew.

And she prayed—not for him to fall in love with her, because that felt selfish—but for his heart to heal enough for him to be open to all of the good things life could bring.

She sighed and reached for her tablet on the coffee table. Since the night of the fire, she'd put off opening it until after the Christmas party. Well, it was after the party.

Wynn's offer to plan Red Hill Springs's festival would help make ends meet in the long run, but it wouldn't get her through the next month. She'd maxed out her credit card and ordered more blank T-shirts, but the state of her bank account combined with the lack of orders just made her feel defeated.

She couldn't wait any longer. With only a few days until Christmas, she had to get her orders out. She opened her email and sat straight up. In shock, she scrolled through dozens and dozens of orders.

How?

Looking closer, it appeared that some of the orders were from the foster moms. They were buying the shirts she'd made that said things like Strong as a (Foster) Mother. But there was another whole group.

Flipping over to Instagram, she looked at her notifications and saw that she'd been tagged by Wynn Grant in a post of her daughter wearing the Future Rodeo Champ shirt.

It had been liked over four thousand times.

What?

She'd been so panicked about making ends meet and now she was, well, *panicked*. How in the world was she going to get these shirts done before Christmas?

Chapter Seventeen

"I still don't know how you did it," Eve said to Wynn as she slid another T-shirt onto the press. The Christmas pop station was playing on her speaker and, as she worked, Eve's feet moved to the upbeat music.

"All I did was post a cute picture of my kid wearing one of your shirts. It's not even a big deal." Wynn hung a recently completed shirt on the clothesline Eve had strung across the room and handed Lacey one that was ready to fold and wrap.

"It's a big deal to me." Eve picked up the lid on one press and peeled back the transfer paper, then lifted the shirt off and passed it to Wynn before going back to the other press and doing the same thing.

"And to me, too. Otherwise, we'd have to find a new tenant. And right now, instead of helping y'all, I'd be up at the house watching some Christmas cartoon on the Baby Channel for the four hundredth time." Lacey folded the finished shirt, slid it into a cellophane bag and sealed it with one of Eve's stickers. "Perfect. I think that's the whole order."

Eve walked over and checked the finished shirts against the order before pulling the receipt and mailing label out of her folder. "Okay, so now we put the shirts in the bag, seal it up, label it and toss it in that box over there with the ones I did last night."

"I'll package these while y'all start on the next order," Lacey said, pulling out one of the cute pink-and-white mailing envelopes and stuffing it with the T-shirts. "So Eve, I think you missed a spot."

"What? Where?"

Lacey laughed. "You could definitely hang some mistletoe from the ceiling fan."

Eve pressed a hand to her forehead. "I thought you meant on the shirt and I almost had a heart attack. Tell you what, you bring the mistletoe and I'll hang it."

"As long as you don't kiss me!" Lacey laughed again.

"I don't think you're the Cole she wants to kiss," Wynn joked, with a sideways glance as Eve's hands suddenly got busier with the heat press.

"What happened with him yesterday?" Lacey took her time straightening the label on the package before smoothing it into place, *not* looking at Eve.

"Something happened with Tanner?" Wynn looked from one to the other. "Okay, guys, spill. What's going on?"

Eve shared a glance with Lacey. "It's nothing, honestly."

Wynn narrowed her eyes. "Not buying it. Does this have something to do with Garrett's big news?"

"He told you?" Lacey asked.

"Of course. We're partners. And more importantly, Abby's my best friend."

Lacey beamed up at Wynn. "Aren't you excited? I'm

over the moon that our baby will have a cousin around the same age."

Wynn patted her stomach under her loose tunic. "I think Red Hill Springs is about to experience a population boom."

Lacey squealed and Eve laughed, both of them crowding Wynn into a hug. "Congratulations!"

"Thanks. We're excited." Wynn's cheeks were pink. "But even baby news is not enough to distract me from my question. What happened with Tanner?"

"Ask Eve. She's the one who followed him when he left." Lacey took the T-shirt Wynn handed her and folded it. "According to Devin, he came back all silent and broody."

"Ooh," Wynn said. "That doesn't sound good."

Eve took her time with the next T-shirt, centering the design carefully. "I'm not sure what to say, other than he's struggling a little with the idea of risking his heart again."

Wynn frowned as she took a shirt off the line. "What does that mean, exactly?"

Looking down at her hands, Eve said, "Well, he said he thought we should stop seeing so much of each other."

"Oh no," Lacey said. "What's he thinking?"

"Self-preservation." Pulling the T-shirt off the press, Eve handed it to Wynn with a shrug. "I get it. When my husband died, I wanted to hide."

Wynn raised an eyebrow. "I'm guessing you didn't, though."

"No. I had Alice and a job I had to go to. But I stopped going out with friends, chitchatting at the coffee shop on the way to work… I even stopped going to church for a while. It's hard to reach out when you're just trying to keep breathing."

Lacey had big tears in her eyes. Eve nipped a tissue from the box on the counter and handed it to her. "Your hormones are showing."

"You didn't ask my opinion, but I'm going to give it to you anyway." Wynn kept their little assembly line going as she spoke.

"Like that's a surprise," Lacey quipped. Then, as Wynn held up a folded fist, she shot both hands into the air. "*Joking.* I'm joking."

Wynn shook her head with a small eye roll. "This is a character flaw I can live with." Turning back to Eve, she said, "My opinion is you should tell him how you feel. You do like him, right?"

Eve nodded, miserably.

Lacey had gone back to work folding and packaging the T-shirts, but she looked up now. "Our esteemed mayor is right on this one. You should tell him. It's never good to keep that sort of thing bottled up."

"It took me a while to work up the courage to tell Latham how I felt, especially since we had some history to work through."

Eve didn't say anything, but in the pit of her stomach, a knot was growing.

"I know what you mean. I was so determined I wasn't going to fall in love with Devin again after he walked out. But then I went and did it, anyway."

Wynn was nodding her head in a big exaggerated motion. "Lay it all out there."

"I told him," Eve blurted.

Both heads swung toward her, the Christmas music sounding loud in the sudden lack of chatter.

"No! You did?" Lacey pressed her fingers to one eye, wincing the other one closed.

"What happened?" Wynn sat down on a kitchen chair. "I'm guessing it wasn't good if he came back, what did you say, Lacey? Silent?"

"Silent and broody," Lacey confirmed.

"I think his exact words to me were *I don't know what you want me to say*." Eve's eyes filled with tears, and she wiped them away, horrified. "Oh, I don't know why I'm crying. I understand him. I get that the number of things he has to care about is growing exponentially and he can't figure out how to handle it."

"Oh, honey." Lacey's eyes were full again, her emotions so close to the surface. "He'll come around. These Cole boys are tough nuts to crack."

"I know. And I'll be fine either way. I always am."

Later, after her two friends left, as Alice played outside on the front porch, Eve worked on the final few orders by herself. She hadn't intended to lie.

She would be fine. Eventually.

Probably?

She just really hoped she wouldn't have to find out.

With the new-old barn shored up with the help of their friends, it was ready for use. Just in time, too. Devin's first client, a barrel racing champion that had suddenly started shying from barrels, was arriving the day after Christmas.

The temperature was warm today. Unseasonably warm for December, but the weather was supposed to take a turn for the worse. Or better, Tanner supposed, if you were one of those people who liked to have cold weather on Christmas.

He set his shotgun against the wall of the barn. Snakes loved hay bales, and as warm as it was today, it was possible they'd be moving. He picked up his pitchfork and started shoveling hay into the large stall where his brothers were arranging it.

"Rain coming in tonight," Devin said.

Garrett groaned. "I'm sick of rain."

"But then the temperature is supposed to drop like a rock. We're gonna have to find coats and gloves for the Christmas Eve service at church tomorrow night."

"I'm not sure I even have gloves." Garrett frowned.

"Next," Tanner said. Devin and Garrett followed him to the next stall. There was a lot of work to do on the farm to make sure the animals would be safe in freezing temperatures. They weren't any more used to the cold than Garrett was. Difference was, animals were more adaptable.

He knew one person who would be overjoyed to have a fire going in the fireplace while she and Alice drank their hot chocolate on Christmas Eve. He'd really messed things up there, a fact he was sure to hear about from Lacey when they sat down for supper tonight. In fact, maybe he'd skip supper tonight.

"You're scowling." Devin's voice broke into his thoughts.

"So?"

"So, you've barely said a word to anyone since yesterday afternoon."

"I'm not chatty. Sue me."

"You're not chatty on a normal day. This is downright sulking. Am I right, Garrett?"

"Uh-uh. Leave me out of this. You kick a hornet's nest, that's on you." Garrett turned his back on the two of them and shoved hay into the corner of the stall with his rake.

Tanner supposed in that analogy *he* was the hornet's nest. Not exactly a flattering comparison.

"What happened yesterday?" Devin never had been able to leave well enough alone.

"Eve told me she loves me." That should shut his brother up. None of the Coles liked to talk about their feelings.

"I hate to break it to you, but that's not as shocking as you think it is. And you said?"

"Nothing." He saw the look that passed between Garrett and Devin. "I'm dealing with it."

Devin scoffed. "Dealing with it by ignoring it? That's real mature."

Tanner took a deep breath and fantasized about punching Devin and knocking the breath out of him so he couldn't talk.

"I'm thinking about it," Tanner muttered.

Garrett stopped and leaned on his rake. "It's not about what you *think*, bro. What do you feel?"

So much for Coles not talking about their feelings. He growled, so annoyed that, for some reason, the truth blurted out. "I *feel* like I've repressed my feelings for so long I don't even know if I have any, okay? You two get married and suddenly turn into Oprah Winfrey?"

"Deflecting." Devin gave Garrett a knowing look, and they both nodded.

"You two are ridiculous. I don't know why I bother talking to either of you." Tanner stabbed the pitchfork into the pile of hay and threw it into the stall.

"Seems like you might be feeling anger, Tanner."

"Yeah, I think you found that one feeling." Devin held out a work-gloved fist, and Garrett bumped it with his, laughing.

Tanner gave up. There was no having a serious conversation with the two of them. He picked up his shotgun from the wall. More than once, his dad had killed a rattlesnake that slithered out of the hay. Seemed like a fitting metaphor for the ambush that had just happened.

The fact that they were right about him avoiding his feelings just made things worse.

He walked out the back door of the barn and whistled for Toby. He was saddling his horse when Devin joined him. "Sorry we ganged up on you. I'm not gonna pester you, I just wanted to give you something to think about."

Tanner buckled the billets one at a time. "I'm listening."

"Just…remember even if you think something's impossible, that doesn't mean it is." His brother waited a moment and then, when Tanner didn't answer him, walked away.

A few minutes later, Tanner was riding out, his shotgun on his lap. He had no idea where he was going. Just away from here. Away from prying brothers, awkward questions and advice that made him think.

Guiding Toby the long way around the property, he skirted the pasture and wound through the woods. It was cooler, more peaceful in the woods. The chatter of birds and bugs wasn't intruding, not like Devin's incessant chatter.

He was able to breathe outside, away from people, but even so, he couldn't seem to clear his head of thoughts of Eve.

He sighed. It was inevitable that he ended up near the cottage. He couldn't seem to stay away. No—the cabin was smack in the middle of his property. Of course he had to pass nearby. He slowed Toby to a stop.

The front door was wide-open. He could hear her singing "Jingle Bells" off-key, at the top of her voice. He shook his head. She was so utterly herself. Funny, energetic, eternally hopeful.

How was he supposed to keep from falling in love with her?

With Sadie lounging nearby, Alice played with her animal figurines in the sandy spot at the bottom of the stairs. She was singing, too, her happy voice drifting back to him.

Sadie lifted her head and growled. Was she growling at him? No, she was looking the other direction, the hackles on her back rising. Her growl grew louder, and she eased to her feet, her attention glued to something he couldn't even see.

And then he heard it. A rattle.

Toby shied, and Tanner fought to keep him under control as the huge muscles bunched underneath him. There. It was small, but no less deadly than a huge snake. And it was close to Alice. Too close.

Thoughts tumbled end over end in his mind. He didn't want to scare her or for her to make a movement that would cause the snake to strike.

His hand closed around the shotgun. He would only have one chance. He edged Toby closer, the horse catching Tanner's apprehension, his feet stomping the ground. Alice's head lifted, her eyes lighting.

Out of time.

"Alice, cover your ears and cover your eyes. *Now.*" He whipped the shotgun up, snapped the barrel into place and fired the shot, all in one smooth movement.

Before the report of the shot had stopped reverberating, he'd vaulted off his horse and to Alice, snatching her up into his arms. Her little body was trembling, but she was alive, unharmed. With a sob, he said, "I'm so sorry, baby. You're safe now. It was a bad snake, but it's gone."

He murmured it over and over again into her hair, soothing her with his voice and his hand at her back, until she stopped shaking. When he looked up, Eve was on the porch, her eyes on him, tears streaking her face.

"A snake?"

"Rattler." He held out his arm, and she stepped into it. He held them both close and let the feeling sink in. The feeling that he wasn't alone. That they were both here and they were both safe.

Alice's head popped up. "Mama, I'm hungry. Can I have something to eat?"

His hands were still shaking, but he laughed as Eve said, "Yes, I think we can make that happen."

He let Alice ease down. "Stay inside, okay, princess?"

"'Kay." Alice ran inside, followed closely by Sadie. He had a feeling neither Sadie nor Eve would let Alice out of their sight for the rest of the day.

"Interest you in a PB and J?" Eve's tone was light, but her eyes were wary.

"I have to go."

Her hand on his arm stopped him, and he raised his eyes to meet her gaze. "Thank you. If you hadn't happened to be here..." She let her sentence trail off, but she didn't have to say the words.

He nodded. "I'll see you around."

Was it possible for a broken heart to hurt even more? Tanner sighed, his thoughts going back to what his brother had said. *Just because you think something's impossible doesn't mean it is.*

Was it really that simple?

Chapter Eighteen

All through the next day, the terrifying moment replayed over and over in Eve's mind, even as she made her traditional Christmas Eve hot cocoa. She'd been in the kitchen singing along to her music, finishing up local T-shirt orders when she'd heard Tanner's voice. A tone she'd never heard from him before.

The gunshot had caught her off guard as she scrambled for the door. She ran toward the sound, stopping short as she saw Tanner vault off his horse, snatch Alice up from the ground and wrap his arms around her. He had tears streaming down his face but was somehow able to keep his voice steady as he soothed her. *You're okay. I'm here.*

The raw, unguarded emotion on his face had taken her breath away. And then, once he'd regained his control, he'd left without any other explanation.

Eve dropped marshmallows into the mugs and stared down as they swirled in the creamy milk chocolate.

She'd just watched him walk away, thanking Jesus that he'd been there and her baby was safe.

What else would she do? She'd told him she loved him. Her heart was in his hands, and she had to be patient. If she had any hope of a future with him, he needed time to figure things out. She couldn't force it. She could choose to give up, maybe. But would that help her avoid heartbreak? No. And besides, she was stronger than that.

She believed he was stronger than that, too, but when she hadn't heard from him all day on Christmas Eve, she'd started to wonder. Maybe she was wrong about him.

Maybe he wasn't ready.

Maybe he never would be.

She picked up the mugs and called Alice. "Are you ready, Ali-Cat? Have your Christmas pj's on?"

Her four-year-old danced out in pajamas decked with her favorite princess and, of course, topped with a matching tulle princess skirt. She twirled to a stop, her little hands in fists on her hips. "Where are your Christmas pj's, Mama?"

"I'll put them on in a little while. Right now it's time for Christmas wishes and hot chocolate by the fire."

"Christmas wishes!" Alice did another twirl in her glittery skirt, blond curls whirling with her. Eve laughed. She'd worried the gunfire would be a setback for Alice, but instead the opposite had happened. Tanner had kept her safe, and that fact seemed to ease Alice's fears.

Eve's worry about having to move had been settled, too. With all her orders packaged and sent—thanks to Lacey and Wynn's help—and her bank account nicely full, her fears of having to uproot their small family again had dissipated.

Eve brought the Santa mugs filled with hot chocolate, placed them on a stool in front of the fire and topped them with a peppermint stick. This was Eve's favorite Christmas tradition. And it wasn't about the decorations or the gifts—it was about the people they loved. "Ready now?"

"Wait, Mama. One more thing." Alice ran for her bedroom, returning in just a moment with the baby Jesus from her grandparents' nativity and a crib from her animal figurine set. She placed the crib under the tree and, very gently, placed the baby in it. "There you go, Baby Jesus. We've been waiting for You to come."

Eve swallowed hard around the knot in her throat. Alice had managed to drill down to the very heart of Christmas with one nativity figure. *Baby Jesus, we've been waiting for You to come.*

Eve settled on their pile of blankets and took a sip of her hot chocolate. Alice flopped down beside her. The fire was warm and cozy, despite the blustery winter weather outside. "Okay, it's time for Christmas wishes. Who are you going to wish for first?"

"The babies."

Surprised, Eve laughed. "Okay, what's your Christmas wish for the babies?"

"I wish that the babies grow up and learn to stop pulling hair."

Not exactly the idea of Christmas wishes since that wish definitely benefited Alice, but Eve decided to give her daughter a pass. "My turn?"

"Yes!" Alice bounced.

Eve pretended to think. "My wish is for Gramma and Grampa—that Gramma would get to bake cookies with you and that Grampa would get to take you for a long walk, because that will make them very happy."

"I like that wish! Now me?"

As Eve nodded her head, there was a knock at the door. Sadie barked. Eve's stomach flipped, heart picking up the beat, even as she told herself not to get her hopes up.

When she pulled open the door, there he was—his dark brown hair with the tinges of gray at the temples, his jeans and boots. His long, lean body topped by the tackiest Christmas sweater she'd ever seen. It was bright red with a neon-green Christmas tree, complete with lights that flashed on and off.

She pressed her lips together so she wouldn't laugh. "Merry Christmas, Tanner."

"Mr. Tanner!" Alice flew to the door and launched herself at Tanner, who caught her handily and settled her on his hip. "It's Christmas Eve. We're doing Christmas wishes."

"That sounds awesome." His slow smile curved in his face, but his eyes, when they met Eve's, were uncertain. "Is it okay if I come in?"

Eve nodded and stepped out of the door so he could enter, pushing it closed against the bitter, cold wind. "I'll get you a cup of hot chocolate. It's our tradition."

He followed her into the kitchen with Alice still in his arms.

As Eve poured another mug of hot chocolate and topped it with a peppermint stick, she said, "That's quite a sweater you have on."

"I've been told I needed to find some Christmas spirit." He set Alice on her feet, and she danced off. "I looked for it. I even felt it, from time to time, but I could never quite get it to stick around. I even bought this tacky sweater before I realized that my Christmas spirit doesn't come from the lights or the tree or the music."

Her eyes filled. "No?"

"No. It took me a while, but I finally figured out it's you. You make me feel something I haven't felt in a long time. *Hope*." He lifted one shoulder, his own eyes glossy. "I didn't know how to handle it. I'm sorry."

She took his hands and looked into his eyes. "That's the most awesome sweater I've ever seen."

He laughed and closed his eyes, letting a long, relieved breath seep out. "You're not mad?"

"No. There's no reason to be," she said simply. "Do you want to do Christmas wishes with us?"

"Ah, sure? Can I take off this sweater now?"

Eve laughed as she settled back into her place on the floor in front of the fire. "I think that would be okay."

Tanner turned off the battery pack and pulled off the crazy sweater, revealing his customary flannel, this one in red and green. Christmassy. She smiled up at him as he sat cross-legged right next to Eve, across from Alice.

He took a swig of his hot chocolate. "So how do Christmas wishes work?"

Alice said, "We take turns picking somebuddy we love and we make a wish for them. Something *they* would like. It's the rules. And it's my turn."

"Okay, then. I'll follow your lead." Tanner's hand crept into the space between them and found Eve's, lacing his fingers through hers.

Eve could barely breathe, let alone follow what Alice was saying, but when Alice announced that she was doing "Mr. Tanner," Eve's attention snapped to her daughter.

"My Christmas wish is that Mr. Tanner could have a family and not be sad anymore."

"Oh, Alice. That's such a sweet wish." Eve watched Tanner for his response, but she needn't have worried.

His gaze on Alice was soft. "That's the sweetest wish anyone's ever made for me." Swallowing hard, he said, "I never expected to find you two. Never expected to want to."

"I certainly didn't expect to move to Alabama and find myself in love with a cranky cowboy."

He laughed. "Well, who can resist a cranky cowboy?"

"Not me, apparently. Okay, it's my turn," Eve said. "My wish is for Alice. I wish that Alice would always be as brave as she is right now."

"I am really brave!" She announced it as if they would be surprised by the fact.

"I wish I had as much courage as you, Alice." Tanner said it quietly. He took a deep breath. "Is it my turn?"

When Alice nodded, he turned to Eve. "My wish is for Eve. I wish that you will always know just how much you're loved." He pulled a small box out of his pocket and handed it to her. "Merry Christmas."

A tear streaked down her face. She opened the box, gasping as she saw the diamond solitaire. Her hand went to her throat. She breathed his name.

"I love you, Eve." He looked at her through a blur of

tears in his own eyes, feeling like his heart might beat out of his chest. "Marry me? Please?"

"We will!" Alice's little voice piped up, and Eve laughed.

He couldn't breathe, waiting for her to answer. "Eve?"

"Are you really sure this is what you want?" Her eyes searched his, looking for reassurance.

"I've never been more sure of anything in my life."

A slow smile started to form on her face. "Alice and I start playing Christmas music in October."

His eye began to twitch. "Still sure."

"We have three Advent calendars."

A small shudder, but—"Still sure."

She narrowed her eyes and said, "All the tinsel—"

Tanner leaned forward, stopping her words with a kiss. As her arms curved around his neck, he said, "I'll put the tree up in August if you want. I don't care. I want us to be a family. Marry me, please?"

"Yes." She laughed. "Yes, I will marry you. *We* will marry you."

Taking the box from her, he tugged the ring out and slid it onto her finger. Cupping her face in his hands, he kissed her.

Tanner turned to Alice and crooked his finger at her. She crawled in between him and Eve, and the two of them together pulled her close. "Do you think you'd be okay with me being your dad?"

His little princess narrowed her gaze. "Does that mean I get to keep Hamlet?"

Tanner laughed. "Why do I have the feeling this is the first of many negotiations I'm going to have with you?"

From his back pocket, he pulled out the picture she'd drawn of the three of them under a rainbow and tucked it into the branches of the Christmas tree. "You know what? I'm pretty sure my Christmas wish already came true."

Eve kissed Alice on the head and leaned forward to kiss him. "Best Christmas ever," she whispered.

Later, after the cookies had been left out for Santa and Alice had been tucked into bed, Tanner sat with Eve in front of the fireplace. She pointed upward, and when he looked, he saw that they were sitting under mistletoe.

He wrapped his arms around her and pulled her close, tipping his head down so he could kiss her properly. When he pulled back, he ran a finger down her cheek. "You are so beautiful. Your heart drew me in from the first day I met you."

"The first day?" Her tone was skeptical.

"Almost the first day," he allowed. "I've been afraid for a long time, so afraid that I didn't let myself feel anything, especially love. But you showed me that love isn't finite. If you share it, it grows. I want to love like that. I want us to love like that."

"You already do, Tanner." She smiled up at him, and in her eyes he could see the reflection of Christmas—love, joy, grace. Second chances.

His heart was so full. It was a revelation to him, that love could find him, even when he was so lost.

And now that they'd found him?

He was never letting go.

Epilogue

～

Christmas night, one year later

Tanner flopped down on the king-size bed they'd wedged into the master bedroom in the farmhouse. "I'll never stop being grateful Devin and Lacey finally got their house built."

Eve was already under the covers, her freshly scrubbed face tired but happy. "Well, they needed more room, too, especially since the little surprise."

The "little surprise" was what they'd taken to calling Liam, the baby who'd surprised them all at Lacey's second ultrasound. Twin B, the doctor had called him. Heart attack, Devin had called him.

"Yeah, four kids under the age of three…" Tanner shuddered. "I realized too late that I should've gotten some earplugs before we opened presents today."

"It was a zoo," Eve agreed. "Abby looked good. Baby Olivia is so sweet."

"Charlotte and Olivia are gonna give their daddy a

run for his money when they get a little older. Did you see Charlotte chasing the goat around the front yard?" Tanner laughed. "It was a hoot. Charlotte chasing the goat, Garrett chasing Charlotte. Abby was just sitting on the porch eating a piece of pecan pie."

"Mom goals," Eve said.

"I checked on Alice. She's crashed out, arms and legs going all directions. Sadie's sprawled out beside her. Both of them exhausted."

"It was a busy day. I've never seen so much food. Or so many presents." She reached to the side and pulled out the drawer on the bedside table. "Which reminds me. There's one more for you."

"But we already opened our gifts to each other." He pulled the paper off and opened the top of the box. "Is this a—it's a—*wait*, this thing says *pregnant*?"

He looked up and realized Eve had big tears brimming in her eyes. "Hey, why are you crying?"

"I know you didn't really want more kids."

Tanner leaned forward and kissed her gently. "Can I tell you something? I'm not scared anymore. I realized that if I spent all my time thinking about what catastrophes could happen, I'd miss all the blessings with all of you. And I don't want to miss a thing."

"I love you so much." She laid her head on his shoulder and snuggled in. "You know what this means?"

"Alice's Christmas wish is going to come true? It was a good day, Mrs. Cole," he murmured into her hair.

"Best Christmas ever," she whispered back.

He kissed her temple. "My Christmas wish for you is that all of your Christmases are the best ever. I love you."

With her head snuggled into his shoulder, she mumbled sleepily, "I love you, too. I wish for you…"

Her voice trailed off, but he smiled. He didn't need any Christmas wishes this year. Because with Eve, all his wishes had already come true.

* * * * *

*If you loved this story, check out
the other books in the
Triple Creek Cowboys series*
The Cowboy's Twin Surprise
The Cowboy's Unexpected Baby

*And be sure to pick up the books
from her previous series,
Family Blessings*

The Dad Next Door
A Baby for the Doctor
Their Secret Baby Bond
The Marriage Bargain

*Available now from Love Inspired!
Find more great reads at www.LoveInspired.com*

Dear Reader,

This story brings us to the end of the Triple Creek Cowboys series. The Cole brothers have a special place in my heart. These brothers were having a hard time seeing God at work in their lives as they were trying to find a way to move on. Forget thriving—separately, they were each just trying to survive.

Saving Tanner's story for last was a deliberate choice. Tanner experienced a tragedy that most of us can't fathom. He was happy for his brothers as they were able to move on with their lives and find happiness. As the brothers began to grow closer, he was able to crack open the door to his heart, just a smidge, to let them in. But even as he saw God at work in his brothers' lives, he didn't really believe that God could restore his own.

He needed a special heroine, one willing to go toe to toe with this wounded hero. One who understood loss and grief but who could show Tanner that, even though you may never stop grieving, joy and redemption is possible. Eve and Alice fit the bill. And slowly, Tanner was able to let go of the past and step into the future.

There are times in our lives when we can't see God's hand at work. *He is still working.* There are times when we can't feel God's presence. *He is still with us.* There are times when we can't understand how God could possibly have a plan for this. *He still does.*

I'm so thankful for you, and I love hearing from readers! Please feel free to email me at steph@stephaniedees.

com or look me up on Facebook at www.facebook.com/ authorstephaniedees and Instagram at www.instagram. com/authorstephaniedees.

With love,
Stephanie

AN AMISH WINTER
by Vannetta Chapman and Carrie Lighte
Amish hearts are drawn together in these two sweet winter novellas, where an Amish bachelor rescues a widowed single mother stranded in a snowstorm, and an Amish spinster determined never to marry falls for her friend's brother-in-law when her trip south for the winter is delayed.

THE AMISH BAKER'S RIVAL
by Marie E. Bast
Sparks fly when an *Englischer* opens a store across from Mary Brenneman's bakery. With sales declining, she decides to join a baking contest to drum up business. But she doesn't expect Noah Miller to be her biggest rival—and her greatest joy.

OPENING HER HEART
Rocky Mountain Family • by Deb Kastner
Opening a bed-and-breakfast is Avery Winslow's dream, but she's not the only one eyeing her ideal location. Jake Cutter is determined to buy the land and build a high-end resort. Can his little girl and a sweet service dog convince him and Avery that building a family is more important?

THE RANCHER'S FAMILY SECRET
The Ranchers of Gabriel Bend • by Myra Johnson
Risking his family's disapproval because of a long-standing feud, Spencer Navarro is determined to help his neighbor, Lindsey McClement, when she returns home to save her family ranch. But as they work together, can they keep their forbidden friendship from turning into something more?

A FUTURE FOR HIS TWINS
Widow's Peak Creek • by Susanne Dietze
Tomás Santos and Faith Latham both want to buy the same building in town, and neither is willing to give up the fight. But Tomás's six-year-old twins have plans to bring them together. After all, they want a mom...and they think Faith is the perfect fit!

AN UNEXPECTED ARRANGEMENT
by Heidi McCahan
Jack Tomlinson has every intention of leaving his hometown behind—until twin babies are left on his doorstep. He needs help, and the best nanny he knows is Laramie Chambers. But proving he's not just her best friend's irresponsible brother might be a bigger challenge than suddenly becoming a dad...

———————

Get 4 FREE REWARDS!

We'll send you 2 FREE Books plus 2 FREE Mystery Gifts.

Love Inspired books feature uplifting stories where faith helps guide you through life's challenges and discover the promise of a new beginning.

FREE
Value Over
$20

YES! Please send me 2 FREE Love Inspired Romance novels and my 2 FREE mystery gifts (gifts are worth about $10 retail). After receiving them, if I don't wish to receive any more books, I can return the shipping statement marked "cancel." If I don't cancel, I will receive 6 brand-new novels every month and be billed just $5.24 each for the regular-print edition or $5.99 each for the larger-print edition in the U.S., or $5.74 each for the regular-print edition or $6.24 each for the larger-print edition in Canada. That's a savings of at least 13% off the cover price. It's quite a bargain! Shipping and handling is just 50¢ per book in the U.S. and $1.25 per book in Canada.* I understand that accepting the 2 free books and gifts places me under no obligation to buy anything. I can always return a shipment and cancel at any time. The free books and gifts are mine to keep no matter what I decide.

Choose one: ☐ **Love Inspired Romance Regular-Print**
(105/305 IDN GNWC)

☐ **Love Inspired Romance Larger-Print**
(122/322 IDN GNWC)

Name (please print)

Address   Apt. #

City   State/Province   Zip/Postal Code

Email: Please check this box ☐ if you would like to receive newsletters and promotional emails from Harlequin Enterprises ULC and its affiliates. You can unsubscribe anytime.

> **Mail to the Reader Service:**
> **IN U.S.A.:** P.O. Box 1341, Buffalo, NY 14240-8531
> **IN CANADA:** P.O. Box 603, Fort Erie, Ontario L2A 5X3

Want to try 2 free books from another series? Call 1-800-873-8635 or visit www.ReaderService.com.

*Terms and prices subject to change without notice. Prices do not include sales taxes, which will be charged (if applicable) based on your state or country of residence. Canadian residents will be charged applicable taxes. Offer not valid in Quebec. This offer is limited to one order per household. Books received may not be as shown. Not valid for current subscribers to Love Inspired Romance books. All orders subject to approval. Credit or debit balances in a customer's account(s) may be offset by any other outstanding balance owed by or to the customer. Please allow 4 to 6 weeks for delivery. Offer available while quantities last.

Your Privacy—Your information is being collected by Harlequin Enterprises ULC, operating as Reader Service. For a complete summary of the information we collect, how we use this information and to whom it is disclosed, please visit our privacy notice located at corporate.harlequin.com/privacy-notice. From time to time we may also exchange your personal information with reputable third parties. If you wish to opt out of this sharing of your personal information, please visit readerservice.com/consumerschoice or call 1-800-873-8635. **Notice to California Residents**—Under California law, you have specific rights to control and access your data. For more information on these rights and how to exercise them, visit corporate.harlequin.com/california-privacy.   LI20R2

*When a city slicker wants the same piece of land
as a small-town girl, will sparks fly between them?*

Read on for a sneak preview of
Opening Her Heart
by Deb Kastner.

What on earth?

Suddenly, a shiny red Mustang came around the curve
of the driveway at a speed far too fast for the dirt road,
and when the vehicle slammed to a stop, it nearly hit the
side of Avery's SUV.

Who drove that way, especially on unpaved mountain
roads?

The man unfolded himself from the driver's seat and
stood to his full over-six-foot height, let out a whoop of
pure pleasure and waved his black cowboy hat in the air
before combing his fingers through his thick dark hair
and settling the hat on his head.

Avery had never seen him before in her life.

It wasn't so much that they didn't have strangers
occasionally visiting Whispering Pines. Avery's own
family brought in customers from all over Colorado who
wanted the full Christmas tree–cutting experience.

So, yes, there were often strangers in town.

But this man?

He was as out of place as a blue spruce in an orange grove. And he was on land she intended to purchase—before anyone else was supposed to know about it.

Yes, he sported a cowboy hat and boots similar to those that the men around the Pines wore, but his whole getup probably cost more than Avery made in a year, and his new boots gleamed from a fresh polish.

Avery fought to withhold a grin, thinking about how quickly those shiny boots would lose their luster with all the dirt he'd raised with his foolish driving.

Served him right.

Just what was this stranger doing *here*?

"And didn't you say the cabin wasn't listed yet?" Avery said quietly. "What does this guy think he's doing here?"

"I have no idea how—" Lisa whispered back.

"Good afternoon, ladies," said the man as he tipped his hat, accompanied by a sparkle in his deep blue eyes and a grin Avery could only categorize as charismatic. He could easily have starred in a toothpaste commercial.

She had a bad feeling about this.

As the man approached, the puppy at Avery's heels started barking and straining against his lead—something he'd been in training not to do. Was he trying to protect her, to tell her this man was bad news?

Don't miss
Opening Her Heart *by Deb Kastner,*
available January 2021 wherever
Love Inspired books and ebooks are sold.

LoveInspired.com